Praise for G. Eldon's first book...

MURDER IN THE ROCKIES

"You too should enjoy this engrossing mystery enriched by Smith's love of Colorado's natural beauty."

—Thomas "Dr. Colorado" Noel, University of Colorado Historian

"G. Eldon Smith has fashioned a ripping good murder yarn about justice in the old West."

—Dick Kreck, Newspaper Columnist and Author

Praise for G. Eldon's second book...

TWO MILES HIGH AND SIX FEET UNDER

"G. Eldon Smith has written another very successful mystery featuring attorney Andrew Coyle."

—Susanne W. Freeman, Author of *Any Train to Somewhere*

"Once again G. Eldon Smith presents an engaging Colorado high country mystery featuring Andrew Coyle and a host of colorful characters."

—Rex Olsen, Author of *Medicine Point* and Other Books

Praise for...

MURDER ON MONEY MOUNTAIN

"Gary Smith has done it again! He's given us an entertaining story that plunges the reader into adventure and mystery in old-time Colorado. Thanks and appreciation from a fellow Coloradan."

—Karen Gerdes, Retired University English Teacher

"Gary Smith's *Murder on Money Mountain* put flesh on the bones of Cripple Creek. As a Colorado native, I knew of Cripple Creek but knew nothing about its history. An enjoyable read as attorney Coyle represents defendants in two separate murder cases. Coyle doesn't deviate from his moral code in an immoral culture."

—Bob Cross, Retired Oil Company Executive

"I sent two of G. Eldon Smith's books as Christmas presents. [I'm] looking forward to the next one."

—Vivian Fausset, Former Weekly Columnist *Longmont Daily Times Call*

"While reading and trying to find who the murderer is, G. Eldon Smith has skillfully intertwined some fascinating history of the early days in Cripple Creek and Victor and a delightful glance of Andrew Coyle's family. An intriguing and fun read and a good mystery."

—Roxie Harper, Retired Public School Teacher

"A delightful read depicting life in a mining town at the turn of the century woven into the interesting twists and turns of an action-packed double-murder mystery. All with a fun family touch."

—Wade Biggs, Retired Writer for *Stars and Stripes*

Murder on Money Mountain
by G. Eldon Smith

© Copyright 2024 G. Eldon Smith

979-8-88824-361-9

FICTION
All rights reserved. No part of this publication may be reproduced, stored in a retrieval system, or transmitted in any form or by any means—electronic, mechanical, photocopy, recording, or any other—except for brief quotations in printed reviews, without the prior written permission of the author.

This is a work of fiction. All the characters in this book are fictitious, and any resemblance to actual persons, living or dead, is purely coincidental. The names, incidents, dialogue, and opinions expressed are products of the author's imagination and are not to be construed as real.

Published by

◤köehlerbooks™

3705 Shore Drive
Virginia Beach, VA 23455
800-435-4811
www.koehlerbooks.com

MURDER ON MONEY MOUNTAIN

A NOVEL OF THE 1890s CRIPPLE
CREEK, COLORADO GOLD RUSH

G. Eldon Smith

VIRGINIA BEACH
CAPE CHARLES

To my three sons,
Scott Alan
Todd Andrew
Brian Austin
One out of three lived a long life.

AUTHOR'S NOTE

What Leadville was to silver, Cripple Creek was to gold. The Cripple Creek Mining District was the home of Colorado's largest and last gold rush. Covered wagons with "Pike's Peak or Bust" painted on their canvas covering flooded the Great Plains. All trails headed toward the district just northwest of the famous mountain, Pike's Peak.

Gold production from the district between 1891-1916, was estimated in 1934 dollars to have totaled $340 million. In 1979, the production from those twenty-five years was estimated in 1979 dollars to have been $700 million; in today's dollars that's $3 billion. At least twenty-eight millionaires were made from the gold of Cripple Creek Mining District—when millionaires were millionaires.

Cripple Creek also provided Colorado with its most famous unsolved murder mystery. The madam of Cripple Creek's most luxurious and expensive brothel was killed under suspicious circumstances the night of a gala Christmas Eve party.

Please read, appreciate, and enjoy *Murder on Money Mountain* for what it is, fiction based on historical facts, and for what is not, a factual account of Colorado's wildest days.

CHAPTER 1

Andrew Coyle looked out of the small train window into the darkness, watching the silver tree trunks flash by as an occasional pine or spruce joined the parade of aspen trees dancing across his line of vision at forty-five miles an hour.

Coyle looked back and studied his wife, Sarah, sitting in the seat opposite his. Her dark brown hair fell carelessly across her forehead as she slept. His almost four-year-old daughter, Leona, stretched out on the seat with her head on her mother's lap. Little Onie, as Leona was generally called, was recovering from scarlet fever, and her mother had wrapped Onie in a quilt. Andrew was relieved to get away from the epidemic in Leadville and to return to the bigger city where he would feel at home.

Coyle, a lawyer, had solved a murder case in Leadville. He and Sarah planned to live in the apartment over the Denver haberdashery where Sarah had grown up until they bought a place of their own. But fate had other plans.

Instead of settling in Denver, they were now back on the train heading toward a small mining community called Cripple Creek.

As the train chugged along to the rhythm of *gotta find a*

home . . . gotta find a home, Coyle's mind drifted back to their arrival at Union Station in Denver. There was a large crowd and confusion on the platform as he tried to find a steward to locate Sarah's oversized trunk and Onie's suitcase.

Sarah's father, Max Meyer, had come running down the platform and waving his arms to get the Coyles' attention. *Not bad for an old guy. He must be over fifty*, Andrew had thought.

"Hello, Mister Meyer, we didn't expect you to meet us here, but I sure am glad to see you. I was going to ask if we could stay in the apartment over the haberdashery," Coyle had said.

"We don't haf time for dat," Meyer said in his broken German accent. "Ve got a phone call from Barton Rosenthal. He vants you to come hurry to Cripple Creek. The train is going to leave soon for Colorado Springs, and you can catch a train in Colorado Springs to go to Cripple Creek. But you must hurry. I'll send your baggage on der morning train," Meyer had said.

"When does the train leave for Colorado Springs?" Coyle had asked.

"Ten minutes ago," Meyer said breathlessly. "But der train is alvays late."

The family dashed across the train station to the loading platform arriving just seconds before the train for Colorado Springs departed.

Coyle's mind returned to the present as he again looked back out of the train window.

"I wonder what Bart's hurry is," Coyle said to himself. "He's always been in a hurry, even back in college."

———— ♦ ————

The train slowed and then started rolling again as Coyle looked around. Most of the other passengers were sleeping. Some were talking to each other. None looked as concerned as Coyle who nervously looked out of the window for the dozenth time.

A lone passenger sitting across the aisle leaned over and spoke quietly so as to not wake Sarah and Onie. "That was the big switch back. That's why we slowed. A freight train tipped over on that horseshoe curve a few weeks ago. It took nearly ten days to get the freighter back upright and on the track."

Coyle nodded and smiled. "Thanks, good to know." Coyle felt a drop of perspiration run down his back.

The engine chugged along with its merry song of the wheels on the rails. Seeing Sarah and Onie sleeping made Coyle envious. Once or twice his head rested on the high back of the train seat, and he nearly nodded off.

"Better stay awake," the stranger across the aisle warned. "We are about to Midland Terminal, the Cripple Creek station. The train stops at Midland to unload city passengers. Then it goes to the mines on up Money Mountain. Most of the night shift miners get on the train instead of walking up the mountain."

"Well, we are getting off at Cripple Creek."

The stranger nodded and continued. "You and your misses don't want to be sitting here when the door opens and that bunch of roughneck miners pile in."

Coyle thanked the stranger and set about waking Sarah. He wanted Leona to sleep as much she could; Little Onie was still sicker than she knew.

Coyle had brought his newly purchased Western hat, and his wife wore her conservative style traveling hat and buttoned her coat. They would not be mistaken for miners.

The train whistled as the conductor announced, "Midland Terminal off for Cripple Creek." The stranger smiled and gathered up his belongings in preparation for the ensuing wild scramble by roughnecks to get seats.

As the train slowed to a mere walking speed, there was a massive explosion.

"*KABOMB!*" The sound of dynamite echoed off of the nearby hills and shook the train. Pieces of the terminal annex and its platform hit the side of the train car, breaking passenger windows.

The air around the platform was filled with screams. Those who were too injured to scream groaned. The locomotive screeched to a stop about three yards short of where it usually halted next to the station platform.

The stranger gestured for the Coyles to follow and did not turn around to see if they were behind him. Coyle, and Sarah holding Onie to her shoulder, followed. Behind them was a stream of others rushing to deboard.

At the front door of the car, they descended from the train and ran up steps onto the platform. Coyle held Onie in his arms to allow Sarah to climb the stairs.

Sarah turned at the top of the stairs and tore away the quilt that was keeping Onie warm. Dropping to her knees she wrapped the quilt around a wounded miner. The man opened his mouth to thank her but was unable to speak as he gasped his last breath. Sarah closed his mouth and pulled the quilt up to cover his face.

She went to the next wounded miner who was in a sitting position holding the bottom half of his leg. Sarah motioned for Andrew to hand over his belt.

"Help!" Sarah's scream was hardly heard above the chaos around her. "Coat and belt," she ordered, pointing at Coyle's overcoat. "Somebody call for some help!"

Coyle obliged, picking up Onie with one arm and pulling off his belt with the other arm. Sarah quickly applied the belt tourniquet around the stump and wrapped Coyle's topcoat around the miner. The miner held his severed leg adoringly until he noticed the shoe was missing.

"Who stole my shoe. I can't work without my shoe."

People, dead or wounded, were scattered atop the loading platform. Amid the moaning and occasional screams and general confusion nobody noticed there was another danger about to engulf the small group of potential passengers.

A piece of hot debris had lodged in the corner of the log building housing the Midland Terminal. In a few short moments, the building was aflame.

Coyle, holding Onie, backed away. The hungry flames quickly devoured the logs of the structure. Little Onie snuggled even closer to Coyle's chest and said, "I'm hot, Daddy."

Coyle turned with his back to the fire. "I'm hot too, honey. Soon as we can find your mother we will get away from this hot place."

Sarah was trying to help a massive miner to get up after being knocked by the blast. Coyle intervened, handing Onie to his wife. "Take her. I'll meet you when I get your friend off this loading platform."

Coyle put the miner's arm on his own shoulder as he watched Sarah leading Onie by the hand, down the short flight of steps to the ground. Then he and the miner started down.

"Are you okay? Any broken bones you know of? I don't see any blood."

"I'm okay," said the miner, "just a little shaky and I'm dizzy."

Ding... ding... ding... The fire wagon's bell was nearly drowned out by the sound of the two horses' hooves pounding on the ground as they pulled the fire wagon. An even louder bell announced another fire wagon coming from another direction. Both fire wagons were followed closely by an ambulance. Neighbors from nearby brought carriages. All of the wounded were given rides to receive medical help at a local hospital.

Coyle left the miner he had rescued with a man who had brought his wagon for transportation to the hospital. "I'll never forget you," said the miner over his shoulder as a volunteer helped the crippled miner into his wagon.

Coyle waved goodbye and turned to find Sarah and Onie. He meandered through the crowd of onlookers, and after several exasperating minutes found his wife and daughter. Coyle was amazed at the number of people at the chaotic scene and how quickly they had arrived.

"Are you two safe? I couldn't find you in this crowd." He hugged both Sarah and Onie, one in each arm.

Sarah said, "Safe and sound, we were waiting for you. I thought it would be better if we didn't move around. I had no idea so many people lived in Cripple Creek, and they are all here. I wish I could have helped more of the wounded."

"You helped plenty. The experts are here now. The best thing to do now is stay out of their way. I was glad the train didn't go any farther forward. We would have been in the middle of the explosion." Coyle kissed both of his best girls.

"I saw the engineer help the coal tender climb down out of the engine," Sarah said. "Somebody said the poor man was hit in the head with a big chunk of coal."

"The engine is heavy enough and made out of iron. He probably would have been safer if he had stayed in the engine," Coyle said.

"That is where he was when the chunk of coal hit him," Sarah corrected.

Coyle shook his head in disbelief. Then he noticed Onie squirming; she needed to be moved out of the cold night air.

As they walked toward the business district of town, Sarah kept saying over and over, under her breath, "Wish I could have done more."

CHAPTER 2

The three Coyles found a huge tent that housed a twenty-four-hour restaurant that served meals for miners on night shifts. On Sundays, the tent hosted church services, which seemed fitting since it was used for a traveling revival gathering.

The manager was kind enough to loan them a blanket and a quilt, which they used to make an uncomfortable bed on the dirt floor in a corner of the tent.

At six o'clock the next morning, the night shift roughnecks came in for breakfast. Coyle had been awake for hours. He roused Sarah who had fallen asleep barely an hour before.

"There is a privy out back and a water tank so you can wash up and feel better. If you comb that curl away from your forehead it will make you look better. I'll return the bedding and get some coffee. Meet you back here."

Coyle gathered up their borrowed bed linens and headed to the day manager's station, now operated by the night manager's wife. On his way he passed a table with four men around it.

"Nice looking family," one commented.

"Thank you. They've had a hard trip so far. But they are in good spirits." Coyle was aware that he might be stretching the definition of good spirits. "Have you gentlemen heard about the dynamiting at the train station?"

"Yah, the Midland Terminal."

Another man at the circle started but was cut off by the first man. The first man said, "We heard the explosion down in the mine while it was happening."

"Why would anybody want to blow up a train station?" Coyle asked. "I heard some of the people on the station platform waiting to get on the train died from their injuries."

From across the table came, "Eleven," a simple and succinct statement, and no further explanation.

Coyle was shocked and aghast. It took several seconds, although it seemed longer, before he could speak. "Again, why would anybody want to blow up a train full of passengers?"

The answer came from a bowed head that could barely make itself heard. "Maybe some union men don't like scabs like us taking their jobs and working for wages that nobody can live on."

"My wife and little daughter are not taking anybody's job," Coyle said. "Yet our car was one car length away from being right in front of the blast."

None of the miners around the table said anything.

The mention of his wife reminded Coyle that he was on an errand. "Speaking of my family, I promised that I would bring them something warm to drink."

As he walked away, he heard a husky voice say, "Pretty little wife you've got there." Coyle ignored the wisecrack and continued to the manager's station door.

"You two look like you are ready for breakfast," Coyle said to Sarah. "Here is a cup of coffee, and a nice, warm glass of milk for Onie."

"I don't like milk," said Onie. She was at an age that she did not mind making her likes and dislikes known.

"It will be good for you," countered Coyle.

"I don't like milk."

"Milk will make you grow up big and strong." Sarah was glaring at Coyle for arguing with Onie.

"I don't want to be big," the girl protested.

"Leona, drink your milk right now. We are in a hurry," Sarah admonished. Onie knew that when she was called by her Christian name, she better do what she had been told to do.

They sipped and chatted about the explosion and fire over the hot coffee. They headed to the exit. At the door of the tent, Sarah stacked their empty cups on a table that served that purpose and drank the half glass of leftover milk. Sarah smiled to herself and placed the glass with the cups.

———◆———

After leaving the tent, they went to the Continental Hotel because the restaurant was open, and Sarah had heard the food was as good as any in Cripple Creek. It had been a long time since they had sat down and had a warm meal. To the Coyles it was delicious. Biscuits and gravy, ham and eggs, hot coffee, and no milk. It must have been sent by angels in heaven to the famished travelers.

Coyle spotted a washroom where they could wash up with warm, nearly hot water. Coyle stopped by the front desk to thank the bailiff for the use of the washroom. The bailiff looked at Coyle with a puzzled smile and then went back to his accounting.

With full stomachs and washed up the best they could, they walked into Barton Rosenthal's office, much to Rosenthal's surprise.

"Andy, how did you get here so soon? I didn't expect you for a couple of more days."

"My wife, Sarah, and our daughter, Leona."

"Glad to meet you, Sarah." Rosenthal looked past Coyle and around

Sarah, and said, "Hello, Leona. Nice to make your acquaintance."

"You can call me Onie. Everyone does."

"We came in on the Colorado Springs train last night." Mister Meyer was in such a hurry for us to catch the train that he didn't tell us much about why you want to see me."

CHAPTER 3

Rosenthal flashed a big friendly smile. Coyle had learned that meant Rosenthal was about to ask for a favor.

"One alum doesn't have to have an excuse to want to see another alum who happens to be an old friend."

Rosenthal dragged out two additional chairs. Sarah took her seat and Onie climbed into her chair and put her head on Sarah's lap. Rosenthal offered Coyle his own swivel chair with a pat on Coyle's back and followed with another big smile. He perched on the corner of his desk with one foot on the floor.

"When I talked to Mister Meyers on the telephone, I explained to him that it was a coincidence that his name is Meyers and the name of the street where all the sporting girls in Cripple Creek live in Myers Avenue." He looked at Sarah. "I'm sorry Misses Coyle. But your father and I had a good laugh about it. Sarah looked straight ahead unsmiling because she didn't want to disturb the sleeping Onie on her lap.

Rosenthal turned back to face Coyle. The big smile was gone.

Coyle thought, *Here it comes*.

"I have a friend who got into some trouble."

"What sort of trouble?" Coyle responded.

"Murder trouble," Rosenthal answered.

Coyle sat up a little straighter and leaned forward.

"She didn't do it," offered Rosenthal.

"Let's start at the beginning. Don't leave out any details that might change my mind. Who was the victim? Who is the friend? And why are you so sure that she is innocent?"

"Opal DuPaulette is . . . was the queen—" Rosenthal stopped speaking and took a quick look at Sarah—queen of the red-light district. Only the prettiest and most expensive girls worked at the Homestead, which was the brothel owned by Opal."

Rosenthal blushed and continued.

"Opal decided to throw a party that would end all parties. It was planned for New Year's Eve. Only the finest of everything, French champagne, Russian caviar, roast pork, and pheasant, you get the idea. Opal even ordered a gown from Paris which cost around two hundred dollars."

Coyle was rolling his pencil back and forth across the table, clearly uncomfortable with Rosenthal's description of Opal DuPaulette's gown.

"Only the richest men in town were invited. It cost a thousand dollars to attend."

"I surmise that you attended."

"Well, yeah, I attended. No one would want to miss a shindig like that."

Rosenthal described what he called the greatest New Year's Eve party Cripple Creek had ever seen.

"My 'friend' Suellen Miller is the new girl at Homestead. Sometimes she sleeps in Opal's room because she does not like to sleep in the bed where she works. That night she went to Opal's room to go to bed," Rosenthal said.

"Was she alone?" Coyle asked.

I didn't see anyone coming or going as long as I was there."

"How long were you there?"

"I was sampling the leftovers from the banquet. We don't get caviar every day in Cripple Creek, you know. At ten o'clock or thereabouts, Suellen excused herself. I had to leave at eleven to catch the eleven-fifteen for Colorado Springs. There is someone there I am fond of. I didn't offer to take her out on New Year's Eve, and miss the party, so I thought I owed it to her to be there at midnight."

You owe others a lot more than that, Coyle thought.

"Suellen did wake up when she heard them singing *Auld Lang Syne*. Then she went back to sleep."

"How do you know that? You weren't there?"

"Suellen told me that was what happened."

"Hearsay evidence."

Rosenthal paused in deep thought and brightened like a man who had discovered electricity.

"I think you can handle this case. You don't think I would invite you here with no place to stay. Have you heard of the Woodward brothers?"

Coyle shook his head no and Rosenthal continued. "Fred and Harry Woodward started the town of Victor, which is here in the district."

"The Cripple Creek Mining District, I assume."

"Yes, the district includes Cripple Creek, Arequa, and Victor. In digging the foundation for a hotel building in their new town they came across a rich vein."

"Gold, no doubt."

"Gold and lots of it. They have been buying up claims and houses to build a monopoly in that part of the district. One of their tenants, a group of prospectors, gave up and moved back to where they came from and left intact the house they were renting. I arranged with Fred Woodward for you to have the house for free as long as you are on the trial. So, you don't have an excuse to not take the trial because you don't have a place to stay in Cripple."

"I'll talk to Sarah, and let you know what we decide in the morning."

After arranging to meet the next morning, Sarah started to help Onie to put on her coat. Onie had no problems with sleeves. Getting buttons in the right holes was a problem.

"I want to do it myself," Onie proclaimed loudly. "I'm a big girl now."

After putting on coats, waiting for Onie, and repeating goodbyes, the Coyle's were ready to depart.

"On the street, Sarah said, "You're going to do it, aren't you?"

"Do what?"

"You know what I am talking about. You are going to take the case and defend that woman accused of murder. I know you. You are going to do it, aren't you?"

"We don't have any place to go. Your uncle and his new bride took our room over the haberdashery. Let's see the house first before we make any decisions. After all the Woodward fellow told Barton Rosenthal that we could use the house as long as I stayed on the case. From what Bart told us, the trial shouldn't last too long."

"Momma, Daddy," Onie interrupted, "when are we going to see the red lights?"

"What red lights?" Sarah said.

"The red lights and the lady who is a queen. They must be pretty lights."

"I thought you were asleep." Sarah was quickly thinking of what else Onie might have heard.

"Just sometimes I was asleep."

"We have to go see the house we might live in for a while," Coyle came to the rescue. Some other time we'll go see some pretty lights."

CHAPTER 4

Much to Coyle's surprise, Sarah liked the house that Rosenthal had arranged. Sarah had lived most of her young life in the apartment upstairs above her father's haberdashery in Denver. She liked the idea of having a house to call her own, even for a little while.

Rosenthal and Coyle talked about sleeping arrangements, their meeting the next morning, and where to have breakfast. The whole time Sarah was looking under beds and at wardrobes where they could hang their clothes. Hopefully, her father had located their luggage and had it transferred to the next day's train.

Sarah was a few steps away from panic, worried that her family's belongings were lost or stolen. What kept her from crossing that line was faith in her father.

He's always reliable, she thought.

Calmly and under control she presented her plan. "Onie and I will go to the grocery store and buy a few things like coffee and the like. Then we will try to find a store that sells brooms."

"And a dustpan," Coyle volunteered.

"You can go to the train station and find our luggage. I guess you can give me five dollars for my part." Sarah's upper lip started quivering and her blue eyes filled with tears that revealed she was not all that calm and collected as she pretended to be.

"Our luggage will be at the train station. You will find them, won't you?" Sarah dabbed at her eyes with her hankie.

"I'm sure everything is there. I'll do my best." Coyle gave Sarah a reassuring smile.

Sarah broke out in a happy smile, "If you don't find my trunk and Onie's suitcase, don't bother to come home."

Coyle was happy to hear her say "home." Home at least as long as the trial lasted.

Sarah put on her hat and started to put on her coat. She called to the empty upstairs, "Onie, we are going to the store. You are going with me. Come, let's get ready to go." After a minute or two, "Onie, I'm waiting to go the store. Please hurry." With a stamp of her foot, "Leona, let's get ready to go." Sarah brushed her brown curl from her forehead. She looked upstairs so that her voice would carry to the upper story. "Onie, are you up there?"

Sarah turned to Coyle and said, "I'll look up here. She likes to play hide-and-seek. You can look outside."

"I'm on my way. She couldn't get far."

In about seven minutes Coyle joined Sarah. She was sitting on the next to bottom step of the flight of steps going upstairs with her elbows on her knees. "Did you find her?"

"If I had found her, she would be with me now. No, I didn't find her." Coyle was getting annoyed. "I guess you didn't find her either."

Sarah sobbed. "She's been kidnapped. My poor baby has been stolen."

Coyle was now more angry than sympathetic. "Leona went exploring and wandered off somewhere. She probably can't find her way back. Crying will not help to find her," he said in one long breath.

"I thought you were watching her." It didn't matter who said it because neither was taking the blame.

Sarah dabbed at her eyes with her handkerchief and then tucked the hankie back up her sleeve.

They separated and went around the house in opposite directions. They met in the backyard.

"No luck. Let's check with the neighbors and the neighborhood," Coyle said as he started away. At the first house to the west Coyle went around to the back looking high and low while Sarah knocked at the front door.

"Hi, I'm Sarah Coyle. We are staying next door for a short time. Have you seen a little girl about four? We seem to have lost her."

"Onie, yes, she is here. She is playing with our daughter, Meg. Her real name is Mable, but she hates that. Please come in."

Sarah spotted Coyle looking around a house nearby. "I found her," Sarah called out. "Onie is fine. She has found a new friend already. I'll meet you back home when you find our luggage."

Sarah was happy to meet a woman. So far all she had met in Cripple Creek were men. Men like Rosenthal. She had nobody to talk to. She waved and smiled most charmingly and then went inside, happy to get out of the cold, relieved that Onie was safe and inside.

She always gets me with her smile, Coyle thought as he started toward the train station. *It looks like Onie is not the only one that has found a friend in Cripple Creek.*

CHAPTER 5

Andrew Coyle found his way to the terminal annex without much trouble, even though it was dark when the train had arrived last night. All he had to do was to follow the building supply wagons and they would lead him straight to the train station, which was undergoing a rushed repair from the blast.

Coyle attempted to describe to a station clerk the large trunk and the small suitcase that hopefully had arrived. He was told that all the luggage for Cripple Creek was sent to the warehouse for storage until the owners came to pick it up.

"If it got here this mornin' that's where it'll be," the station clerk said curtly, pointing while reciting the number of city blocks to reach the warehouse. He ended with, "You can't miss it."

On his way out, Coyle passed the next customer in line and said out of the corner of his mouth, "Good luck."

Coyle walked several blocks in the direction the clerk indicated. He passed a group of well-dressed women, stepping off the sidewalk and tipping his hat. A short distance farther he encountered two more woman and tipped his hat, and in the process, he looked past the pair and saw a young woman sitting in the window wearing what looked like a nightgown. Coyle realized he must be on Myers Street, and those friendly young ladies were not ladies at all. Despite his ambivalence, Coyle felt flattered by the women's flirtations. He looked up and noticed the train station warehouse right where the train station clerk had said it would be.

The train tracks ran behind it and the large building held a ton of steel rails and engine parts, everything you would need to build a railroad from scratch.

"See anything you like?" said a warehouse clerk who looked like he was trying to dress better than a warehouse clerk but didn't know how to do it. The striped tie did not go with the plaid flannel shirt.

"I came to pick up a blue trunk and a brown leather suitcase. They were supposed to be shipped here from Denver by way of Colorado Springs. My wife, child and I rushed to catch the train leaving Denver and had to leave our luggage behind. We got in on the train last night when the explosion happened."

"Such a tragedy," the warehouse clerk said. "I need to remind you, it was the train station that was the target, not the train."

"They were both hit very hard, as far as I could see, but we were a couple of yards back from the explosion. The blast might have destroyed the passenger car if the engineer hadn't stopped in time."

"Glad you and your family weren't hurt. Quite a few miners were injured or killed," the clerk said. The clerk pointed at the corner where some luggage was piled together.

"Should be easy to find your trunk and bag. Most people came to claim their own earlier. I was just thinking that you didn't look like a railroad man. If you want anything else," he nodded across the street, "I can make arrangements for you. No haggling when you get there."

"Just the luggage," Coyle said over his shoulder as he walked away toward the corner where the luggage was piled.

"There is a man with a wagon, hanging around for somebody that needs a hand with their luggage. You can wake him up. He don't mind. The horse is a bit touchy if he's napping."

---◆---

After dragging the luggage out of the warehouse and, with help, getting the trunk up and loaded into the wagon, Coyle sat next to the driver who was personable and older, with a chewing tobacco stain on his beard.

The wagon was comfortable as wagons go. The day was warm, but not too hot. Every once in a while, Coyle got a glance at Pikes Peak in the distance. It was not as close as it had appeared yesterday on the train ride into town.

After a couple of generalizations, exchanges of names, and the address where Coyle wanted to take the luggage, they were off.

"Been here long?" Coyle asked.

"Born in the Springs and worked as a cow puncher up here during the summers after I was ten. When I was in my sixteenth year, I met a woman I took a shine to and got hitched. I been punchin' cows, haulin' freight and prospecting ever' since."

"Doing any good prospecting?" Coyle asked, curious about get rich stories he was hearing. *Why not me?* creeped into his conscious, and *maybe someday* into the shadows of his subconscious.

The driver answered. "Bob Womack was a cowboy of sorts when he wasn't looking for gold. I rode by those same hills over by Poverty Gulch where your house is. Didn't find a thing. Sometimes when the mood strikes me, I go over there, and I still don't find anything." The storyteller chuckled. "At least not gold. Womack was systematic about it and had a map which had blocks of land. He'd color in the block he visited that day. One day in '86 he came by a block he had staked a claim on before.

"He checked around and found a few specks of gold that we call floats. He followed a trail of floats to a crack in an underground sandstone formation. Womack and his dentist formed a partnership. The dentist borrowed enough to develop the claim and after a few months in the winter of 1890 Womack found his gold mine. After years of prospecting. Damn, it could have been me."

Coyle looked around at the scrub oaks and occasional outcroppings and heaved a mighty sigh. He said with genuine sympathy, "You never can tell. Don't give up."

Upon getting Sarah's blue trunk and Leona's brown suitcase through the front door, the wagon driver took off with two new quarters in his pocket. Sarah appeared, and Coyle's illusions of prospecting for gold faded away.

Coyle mumbled something about not spending all of the fee he had earned in the Leadville case.

CHAPTER 6

"Good morning, Bart. Who am I going to see today? I hope it is someone that had a motive to murder Opal DuPaulette. Someone who saw Opal after my client did."

"If it was that easy, Suellen wouldn't need a big-time lawyer like you." Rosenthal laughed, letting Coyle know he was just teasing.

Coyle smiled and shook his head.

"I'm busy today. I suggest you talk to the richest man in town. You'll never get him into a courtroom, but he may tell you something from home that you can use."

"Who is that?" Coyle asked.

"Winston Sullivan, the owner of the Declaration mine on Money Mountain. He will be glad to tell you about his mine and how he found it. If you ask him the right questions and listen to him carefully you will get something out of him."

"Like who killed Opal DuPaulette?"

"Like he was her friend. He never went to Old Homestead House that I know of. But he did send for her, and she would go to his cabin close to the Declaration diggings."

"How do you know he won't answer a subpoena?"

Rosenthal chuckled as he thought of a clever retort. "I said he is a very rich man. Somebody that rich doesn't live by the same rules as you and me." Rosenthal looked like a bright idea had occurred to him.

"Here is an example of what I was saying. The city held a big shindig to honor Sullivan after he donated a sizable amount to build a Colorado Springs hospital. They rented a big hall, invited the town millionaires, although there were not as many as there are now, put together an elegant dinner, and a band from Denver."

Rosenthal paused to gather his thoughts. "The only thing missing was Sullivan. Millionaires danced, ate dinner, and sang 'a jolly good fellow,' and went home." Rosenthal looked up, "You still think he will come to trial?"

Coyle answered right away. "How do I get to his house?"

"Catch the morning freight train. They make a loop around Money Mountain to load ore at the mines, then head down to the Springs. The conductor will stop the train both ways, going and coming, if you wave him down."

"Thanks, I'll let you know if he is a jolly good fellow or not," Coyle said as he gathered his things to go.

"I'll call Sullivan and tell him you are coming, and you just want information," Rosenthal said.

"Mister Sullivan, I'm Andrew Coyle, attorney, representing Suellen Miller, whom I understand you know."

"I've heard of her. We don't travel in the same circles."

Winston Sullivan looked to be older than Coyle had envisioned. He wore a black suit and tie, although there was nobody else around. Sullivan had a graying thin mustache, and his head was covered with neatly trimmed gray hair.

"In this spring weather, you never can tell when you will need a vest," Coyle said to open the conversation.

"Makes a good place to carry my watch." Sullivan pulled a watch out of his vest watch pocket. "You've got half an hour. You used three minutes so far and twenty-seven are left."

Coyle perused the papers in his briefcase, knowing there was nothing of value there. He wished he had jotted down some clever questions during the train ride up Money Mountain.

"I'm going to have a drink." Sullivan stood. His shoulders were rounded, but otherwise he appeared to be in good shape. Holding up a whiskey bottle, he asked, "You want a drink?"

"No thank you, Mister Sullivan. But I was wondering about the banquet in your honor in Colorado Springs. Why didn't you go?"

"Those female ditties. I built more than half of their houses. They didn't have any problem complaining and making suggestions. They knew what to say when I was just a carpenter. Now that I have more money than all of them put together," he squeezed out his imitation of a woman's voice, "oh dear, I wouldn't know what to say."

Sullivan did his version of a curtsy and nearly fell over. He did not spill a drop from his glass or the bottle. "I don't like women." He drained his glass in one pull and poured another drink.

"I didn't like my nine sisters, and I still don't like having women around me. My father was a master carpenter in Ohio. He always took my sisters' side. One day he just pushed too far. I ran into the house, picked up his rifle and took it outside. I took a shot at him. I don't know to this day if I hit him or anything, but I didn't think it was a good idea to hang around and find out."

"So you became a carpenter in Colorado Springs?"

"Eventually. With a couple of stops along the way. In the winter I did enough carpenter work to have a grubstake for the summer months. I did that for damn near forty years. Been prospecting in all parts of Colorado and some in Utah. Forty years of tramping up an' down these here hills."

"You called for Opal DuPaulette. She came out here, and you didn't go into town to see her?"

"I didn't need to. She was a good businesswoman. She went where business called."

"And did she—" Coyle paused and might have blushed a few years earlier, but he was over that now. "Did she conduct business when she was here?"

Sullivan pulled his watch from his vest and let it swing from its golden fob. "Times up."

It was not close to the promised thirty minutes, but Sullivan made it clear that the interview was over. Coyle nodded and reached for his briefcase. "Maybe we can talk again sometime soon."

As he picked up his papers and readied himself to go, Coyle said, "Did Opal ever say anything about Suellen Miller?"

"She didn't trust Suellen. But then Opal didn't trust any of her girls, but she especially didn't trust Suellen."

Coyle stepped out into the bright sunlight. It would be a while before the train would take on the ore from the mines from higher up on Money Mountain. He decided to have a look at the Declaration mine that made Sullivan a multi-millionaire.

———•———

"Hi, are you the mine manager?"

"Leon Redd."

"Andrew Coyle. I'm a lawyer in the Opal DuPaulette trial. I've been talking to Mister Sullivan at his home yonder up the hill."

"So?"

"So, for starters if you would point that rifle some other direction, I would greatly appreciate it."

Redd flashed a guarded smile, breaking the scowl he routinely wore. He pointed the muzzle to the ground but kept his finger inside the trigger guard.

Coyle continued, "I thought you might be able to add some information that would help us find out what happened that night that Misses DuPaulette died."

"Thought you might be with the union." Redd propped his rifle next to the door of the mine office shack. "Come on in. The wind is cold even on a sunny day. Not many trees this high up, and the wind blows all the time."

Coyle was secretly glad to be invited in. For the first time he regretted losing the coat Sarah had given to that poor soul who lost his leg in the explosion at the train station.

"So, you talked to Winston. What did he have to say?" Redd asked.

"He said there was a celebration honoring his good works." Coyle thought he should get into the murder case slowly. Besides Winston Sullivan had not told him anything.

"Yah, any prospector down on his luck can come to Winston and count on a hundred-dollar loan," Redd snickered. "Most of them never come back. A couple have come back for a second helping. Winston just sends them over to see me for a job. As mine super, I can tell you not many last more than a couple of days." Redd leaned back.

"Loans? No pay back? Mister Sullivan did not strike me as that kind of businessman."

"Charity is one thing. If we are talking business that is a whole different story." Redd looked up and tilted his head toward the window. "Sounds like the morning train back to Cripple. Go to the loading chute. They will stop there, and you can ride in the passenger car up front."

Redd walked with Coyle to the front of the mine shack so he could point out where the train would stop. As they stepped out the door, a shot pierced the silence. The sound echoed off the rocks of the adjoining mountains. Redd fell without a sound. Redd's rifle was still propped up where he had left it by the door.

Coyle's long legs took him to a pile of discarded mining debris where he took cover. He heard a locomotive somewhere in the distance. The locomotive came into view and stopped at a spot between Coyle and where he had heard the shot come from. He ran to the entrance of the mine.

"Somebody come up! Mister Redd has been shot. Somebody come up! We need help!"

Slowly the big wheel that operated the pulley that raised the elevator started to turn. A platform crowded with miners appeared after minutes that seemed like hours to Coyle.

He returned to the prone mine superintendent and stuffed a clean handkerchief into the bloody hole on the right side of Redd's chest.

One of the miners that Coyle later learned was the shift foreman grabbed Redd's rifle and took cover behind an ore wagon. The foreman paused. Coyle was sure it was not long enough, but the foreman jumped up and ran in a zigzag to the train. The engineer leaned out of his window and pointed downhill.

"The person you want went over there. I saw the guy, a little guy with a gun. Went that way, away from the train. You'll never catch 'em now."

CHAPTER 7

The shift foreman looked disappointed when he returned to the office shack in front of the mine entrance. He put Redd's rifle in the shack and returned to where Coyle was busy making a stretcher with two-by-fours. "Somebody get a hammer and nails. We can use the blanket. Not the best stretcher, but it will do," Coyle said as he put down the hammer.

"Somebody. You there," pointing at the youngest looking miner, "go up to the house and tell Mister Sullivan what happened."

The youth asked, "What did happen?"

"Let's get Redd onto the stretcher," Coyle insisted. Some looked toward the train as though they thought the shooter might jump out and start shooting again. "Two men on that end and the foreman and I will get this end . . . now!" Coyle looked at the youth and said, "Somebody tell the lad what happened."

In the train, the conductor brought a first aid kit and Coyle tried to remember how the college doctor taped him up after a football injury. He had been sitting in the stands watching the game when a ball hit him in the head. He fell out of his seat and cracked some ribs.

With plenty of tape and gauze from the first aid kit, he temporarily stopped most of the bleeding.

"What is your name?" Coyle asked the man helping to carry the stretcher "I can't call you the foreman all the way to Colorado Springs."

"Marvin Goodson," said the foreman. "Redd is breathing easier. He looks more relaxed too. Think he'll make it."

"We won't know until the doctor gets the bullet out. Probably fifty-fifty chance, Marvin. I reckon they will need a new mine supervisor, either way it turns out."

"Not the reason I asked, Mister Coyle. I'm hoping we catch the shooter and he's charged with murder."

"You're late," Sarah scolded. "I hope you got some supper somewhere."

"I met the supposedly richest man in the Cripple Creek Mining District today."

"That's nice. I got to know our next-door neighbor better today. Her name is Katie, and her husband is John, and they have a little girl named Mable, but everyone calls her Meg. That prompted Leona to say her name is Leona, but everybody calls her Onie."

"It is convenient, they speak the same language," Coyle joked.

"Katie is awfully nice. She said she would take me shopping and show me which items cost less and we can fill up on them and which items are rare and therefore cost more."

"The law of supply and demand," Coyle said dismissively.

"Katie said that prices have come down since the railroad came to town. I told her that we were on the train that came in when the dynamite went off."

"Does Katie know, or does she know anyone who knows who is

behind the explosion?"

"Katie said that John is prospecting in Poverty Gulch and doesn't talk to many people. But she did say she heard about fights between union men and scabs. One mine union manager was shot on Money Mountain, and everybody thinks it was scabs that done it."

"The man I met is named Winston."

"Katie said there has been lots of trouble between the union men and the people that took their place. I'm sure glad you didn't get mixed up in the union mess. One murder, an unfortunate one at that, is the most we want to take on."

Coyle looked at Sarah with an *if you only knew* expression.

The next day, Coyle stopped at the county clerk's office to be sure he was registered as the counselor for the defense. Coyle shook his head when he learned his fellow alumnus had already taken care of it. When he said to the clerk, "Lawyer for Suellen Miller," everyone in the little office stopped talking. A group of four of them moved several inches closer to him.

Coyle spoke up. "Yes, we are sure Miss Miller did not kill Opal DuPaulette. She is a very sound sleeper and therefore does not know who did the deed. I personally ascribe to the theory that Opal DuPaulette overdosed on morphine. Morphine and champagne do not mix. We are waiting for the medical examiner's report to learn whether Opal accidently killed herself."

He turned to the assembled crowd and announced, "You can quote me on that."

Joshua Zigler Funeral Parlor was next door to the county clerk's office. Coyle dropped in with his winter hat in his hand and his suit jacket turned up. He got a look from the undertaker suggesting that Zigler was thinking Coyle was the bereaved and was broke.

"Mister Zigler, I assume. I am the attorney for Suellen Miller. I just stopped to see if the medical examiner had finished with his examination of the deceased, Misses DuPaulette."

"Yeah, he was done a couple of days ago. Normally we don't keep them this long, but we are expecting a visitor. Plus, we had the people that were killed in the explosion at the terminal annex. Did you hear about that?" Zigler looked uncomfortable in his coat and tie, but he had convinced himself that was the uniform of the occupation, and he made the best of it.

"My family and I were on that train. It was quite a welcoming party. I don't think my little girl will get over it. I know my wife and I will always remember that night." Coyle looked down as images flashed across his memory.

Quickly Coyle's head popped up. "Who do you think planted the dynamite?"

Zigler smiled briefly. "Most of my customers don't talk to me. But I've heard some of the survivors say it was the union miners out to get the scabs who were boarding the train for Money Mountain."

The little bell that hung over the door rang. Coyle stepped back into a secluded corner. A woman fashionably dressed but wearing too much makeup strolled into the reception area.

"I'm Miss Beatrice Peterson. I'm looking for my sister Olivia. People in Denver said I might find her here. In letters she said she was a fashion designer and seamstress. I don't know why they sent me to this dump."

Zigler responded. "On the death certificate the legal name of the woman in the backroom is unclear. It would be a great help if you could positively identify her."

Zigler and Miss Peterson walked to the back room. A few minutes later came a scream followed by mournful groans.

Miss Peterson stomped out of the backroom. "Fashion designer and seamstress. My arse."

Zigler appeared in time to hear the little bell over the door rattle as the woman slammed the door behind her. He looked at Coyle and whispered, "Her own sister didn't even offer to pay some of the funeral expenses."

Coyle glanced through the door to the backroom. He briefly saw the body, white ball gown, and the red hair.

"Couldn't miss that beautiful red hair," he muttered half to himself but loud enough for Zigler to hear.

CHAPTER 8

"Good morning, Barton, you're up early this morning," Coyle said with a welcome but cautious smile.

"Haven't been to bed yet. Been out with The Society and got carried away."

"The Society?"

Rosenthal was still having trouble speaking clearly.

"Just a bunch of guys who finished high school and beyond. We don't hold it over anybody just because most of these mining folks only went to eighth grade, or less." Rosenthal chuckled to himself, *'Course we do.*

"So?"

"So people round here say we think we are high society cause we went to college and are doing well financially. So we call ourselves 'The Society.' That's so what."

Coyle smiled. "You better go to bed so you and The Society can have another meeting tonight." He stood to leave Rosenthal's office.

"Wait, Andy. I meant to tell you something." Rosenthal took off his tie and jacket. "Yesterday I bailed Suellen out of jail. She promised not to go anywhere. Said she doesn't have any place to go to. Thought you ought to know." Rosenthal rested his head on his crossed arms on his desk.

"And I meant to tell you that Winston Sullivan is going to be looking for a new mine supervisor. The super got shot at and wounded at the Declaration yesterday. That Leon is a good man. I'm taking the train down to the hospital in Colorado Springs to see if he is going make it."

Coyle made some routine calls with few results, then decided to go back to the rented house and check in on Sarah. It was too nice of a day to be stuck indoors watching Leona.

"Hello, I'm home. Where are my two girls?"

No answer. He climbed the steep staircase. Still no answer. Backyard, and up and down the street. While standing in the middle of the street, Sarah and Onie came around the corner accompanied by Katie and Meg.

"Sorry for the trouble, Katie."

"It was Meg's fault. I am the one who is sorry," said Katie.

"We'll keep a closer eye on them in the future. Bye," Sarah said.

Curious but courteous, Coyle gave Sarah a peck on the cheek. He stood back and silently looked for an explanation. "Wait until we get in the house," she huffed.

In the kitchen, Onie stood aside not knowing if she should cry or not. She evidently decided tears would not help this time.

Sarah faced Coyle with her hands on her hips. Coyle could hear her foot tapping on the floor under her long skirt.

"Do you know what your daughter did?" Sarah said through clinched teeth.

Coyle knew it must be bad. "I was hoping to find out," he stammered.

"Onie knows she can play in this yard and next door but stay where I can see her. Never, never cross the street." Coyle felt like Sarah was lecturing him. "Six-year-old Meg says it is okay because she is older. Meg knows that in the alley there is a backdoor that is open on hot days. They went to the backdoor of Zigler Funeral Parlor. They go trapsing in so Onie could see a dead person. Zigler called Katie and told her there were kids there that he didn't want in his place."

Onie interrupted. "She looked like she was sleeping. She had a pretty white dress and beautiful red hair. But the hair fell off . . . it was not real. The lady had gray hair like Grandma."

Coyle stifled a laugh by biting his tongue, but he could not keep his red mustache from dancing. Sarah turned to give Onie an angry look and then glared back at Coyle with spears in her stare.

Coyle could not hold it any longer. "She fooled me, too," He blurted out between laughs.

"The dead lady used to work at the place where they have red lights," Onie said.

Sarah couldn't fight it, so she joined them in the first hardy laugh they had had together in days.

CHAPTER 9

The day was rainy. Coyle could not figure out the Colorado weather. Not only did it change daily, but often afternoons were completely different from mornings.

A borrowed umbrella that Sarah provided kept Coyle reasonably dry, but a pink umbrella didn't do much for his self-image. He kept the list of names of party attendees that Rosenthal gave him in his briefcase, so that was dry. His boots stayed dry, too, as long as he stayed on the boardwalk.

"Hello, Fred, I almost didn't see you with this umbrella over my head."

"Mister Coyle, I trust the house Mister Rosenthal arranged for you is satisfactory?"

"Here, Fred, step under the umbrella. I was getting half wet anyway. Now both of us will get half wet."

"Don't bother, Mister Coyle. I have a meeting and I am late."

"Bart Rosenthal gave me a list of people at Opal DuPaulette's New Year's party. I think your name was on the list."

"Not me. I was not at that or any other party. My wife was sick, and even if she was well, I still wouldn't have spent that much for a silly party. My brother Harry would have gone. He is one of The

Society boys. Good day, sir."

"Sorry to stop you in the middle of the street in the rain, Mister Woodward. Good day, sir." Coyle tipped his hat. When his hand touched the brim much of the water ran down and into his upturned sleeve.

"Damned pink umbrella," Coyle muttered.

The first name on the list was an employee at the Old Homestead House. Coyle's eyes scanned down the list of those attending Opal's party. Not surprisingly, the first six names were also employees at Old Homestead.

Being ushered into the parlor of the Old Homestead House, Coyle started to question his ability to focus. He had been warned that Madam DuPaulette only hired the prettiest girls, but he didn't expect this.

No place this side of heaven will have so much feminine beauty in one spot, he thought.

Two of the young women had just returned from shopping and were dressed in their finest, donning New York hats to their Paris inspired dresses, and their Italian-styled shoes. Others who looked like they had just woken up wore an assortment of robes over their nightgowns, all looking like the models he'd seen in stereo-scope slides while in college.

Coyle turned to the woman who was filling in for Opal DuPaulette as assistant madam until the courts settled who would assume ownership of the Old Homestead.

"I'm representing Suellen Miller, who has been accused of killing Opal." He turned slightly to have his back to the audience. "By the way, I didn't see Suellen when I came into Homestead. She hasn't left town, has she?"

"No, on advice, she is up in her room. Acting bossy and too good to talk to any of us, as usual."

"We could use some privacy," Coyle said.

The assistant madam shook her longish brunet hair and brushed it back to keep it out of her eyes. "My name is Cora. See anything you like?" Getting no answer, she said, "Let's talk in the kitchen. There's no one there now."

"Suellen can be plenty snooty, but with the customers she is sweet as pecan pie," the madam said.

"Any regulars?"

"We've all got regulars. She had four or five. They all thought they were her one and only. The one she liked and spent time with when she wasn't workin' was Barton Rosenthal."

"What about Opal? Did she have any regulars?"

"She was the owner and madam, so she didn't do tricks." Cora gave Coyle a *don't you know anything* look. "Opal had a boyfriend who she gave haircuts . . . among other things, of course," the madam scoffed.

"And who might that be?"

"Mister Sullivan didn't need that many haircuts. She indulged him 'cause she thought she could get him to pop the question. I say he just wanted free haircuts."

Coyle spoke with a few other of the Holmstead women. All he gleaned was mostly gossip, nothing worth discussing at the trial. He substantiated that Suellen Miller was not generally liked and that Barton Rosenthal was more than just a physical friend and client. He was told that Opal enjoyed the New Year's Eve party immensely and did not charge fees that evening, but the tips were good. Most agreed Madam DuPaulette always had time when Winston Sullivan called. But none had actually seen him.

Despite not getting much useful information, Coyle seemed to enjoy mingling with the women, but he kept a professional demeanor, knowing that his college buddy Bart would hear about any flirtatious behavior. And God help him if Sarah heard such rumblings.

Coyle grabbed his notepad and stuffed it in his briefcase. The rain had stopped, so he did not need the drenched pink umbrella. The umbrella—he had forgotten it. When he ran back and knocked, Cora answered the door.

"Forgot what you came here for?" Cora chided. There were peals of giggles from the parlor.

Before he got the word umbrella out, there was a shot. It was followed by two more.

"Fire, three shots in the air," Cora said. "There is a fire in town!" Three more shots.

———◆———

Coyle ran down Myers Avenue following the others sprinting toward the scene. The ever-growing crowd passed by hastily built buildings that housed dance halls like the Tropic, Red Onion, and Bucket of Blood. Coyle noticed smoke in the air as they passed the Butte Opera House.

At Myers and Third Street was a building with two junk stores and the Central Dance Hall upstairs on the second floor. The wood-frame building went up in flames almost instantly. Only three minutes after the dreaded three shots had been fired, the building looked like a giant torch.

Some of the girls on the third floor stuck their heads out of the windows and screamed for help. They were trapped by the flames. Firefighters took turns throwing ropes up to the hysterical women. In a short time, there were enough ropes for almost everyone to escape. The ones waiting their turns dropped their cats and other small pets to friends below.

Some climbed hand over hand down the anchored ropes. Most let go at about half or three quarters of the way to the ground.

After half an hour the water pressure gave out and the fire hoses were useless. A woman screamed as she ran out of Dorsey Drugs. Her hair and dress were on fire. Coyle tackled her and tried to put sand and gravel on the woman's head to smother the flames. A woman ran over to assist, wrapping a blanket she carried around the victim. Coyle stood after the fire on the burned woman had been extinguished.

"My face, it burns. I can feel the burns. My face, I know it is burned. No man will want me now," the woman sobbed.

"She only wanted to buy some burn ointment," said the woman who brought the blanket. "We thought this building was safe. The fire was three buildings away. Everything happened so fast."

Coyle backed away. He murmured, "I'm sorry." Nothing else seemed appropriate.

Soon, a bucket brigade formed, with men scooping water from the town reservoir and handing them down a chain to someone dousing the flames. Coyle was in the middle of the bucket line working harder than he ever had, but freshly filled buckets were not arriving fast enough to contain the blaze.

Soon, a fire wagon, pulled by two horses, rumbled onto the scene. Shortly after, the firefighters used all the water carried in a large tank on the fire wagon. The Central Dance Hall fire still burned despite the firefighters' best efforts.

About that time the gentle south breeze picked up and floating embers carried in the wind spreading the conflagration. One-woman cribs next to the row of parlor houses were the first to go. Sporting houses went next. Then the fire jumped over to Bennett Avenue, consuming other buildings indiscriminately. Nolon's Saloon, Cripple Creek Mining Exchange, the post office, and the First National Bank all suffered from the inferno. In only three hours the fire left a wasteland of charred, smoldering, wreckage of businesses and dwellings.

Coyle spotted Sarah before she saw him. She was looking at each despondent face in the disbursing crowd. Her frantic search was rewarded when Coyle stepped out from behind the man standing in front of him.

Sarah ran to him and nearly knocked him over. He hugged her closely. At times that morning he felt like he would not see her again.

"What are you doing here?" Coyle asked.

"Looking for you, you big dope. I knew you would try to help. Why didn't you come home to take care of your family?"

"Where is Onie?"

"At Katie and John's house. They are keeping their house safe like you should have been at our house." Sarah continued hugging Coyle and crying into his sweaty shirt.

CHAPTER 10

Life continued at a more frenzied pace. Cleaning out the debris and starting replacements for the burned buildings put craftsmen from Colorado Springs to work. This time bricks appeared where tarpaper and wooden frames had been the norm. Abandoned mines made convenient holes to dump charcoal and partially burned timbers.

Rose Townson had two crews of ten men each building one-woman cribs in a row where previous ones had stood. *The Cripple Creek Times* managed to move to a small job press and published their Sunday paper on time. Lumber was being delivered to a now empty lot where Nolon's Saloon had stood as an anchor on Myers at Third Avenue. A piano player beat out "Roll Out Our Barell" as carpenters pounded nails to build walls for a new saloon.

Cripple Creek Sheriff O'Mally hauled in a bartender and his girl for questioning. After a short time, the dance hall girl confessed, and the bartender corroborated her story and admitted that they had started the fire at the Central Dance Hall. The bartender described how they had argued, and he slapped the girl. She had attacked him with a knife. During their scuffle, a kerosene heater was knocked over, starting the fire.

"Well, as long as no one was hurt with the knife, and you two are not fighting any more, I guess you can go now," O'Mally said. "This was a horrible accident. You two are lucky no one died."

Coyle was in the next room waiting to see the sheriff and had heard the whole exchange. Coyle raised his eyebrows and shook his head.

"Next, come on in," O'Mally called to Coyle.

The sheriff was leaning back in his office chair and spun halfway around to face the attorney.

"Good morning, sheriff. I'm Andrew Coyle, and I'm representing Suellen Miller."

O'Mally pointed at a chair and gestured for Coyle to have a seat.

"Opal DuPaulette was a kind and generous person. Her death was a real loss to this town. She went into business and sold the only thing she had to sell. She was a good businesswoman."

"I noticed you said her death, but you didn't use the word murder."

"I'm only the sheriff. I work for the district attorney. I use whatever words he tells me to. So, I arrested the person considered a prime suspect, and you, Mister Lawyer, bailed that person out. I'm just waiting for the people who are at a higher pay scale than me to weigh in."

"Did you see any signs that Miss DuPaulette took morphine or lithium?" Coyle asked.

"Out a' my pay range, Mister Coyle. You have to ask the county medical examiner." O'Mally spun his chair and when he came to a stop, he had a smirk that reminded Coyle of a kid that had just slipped some vegetables to the dog under the table.

Coyle could see he wasn't going to get any more information out of the sheriff. O'Mally was clearly stonewalling. Coyle pressed.

"You took it pretty easy on those fire starters, sheriff. You just let them go."

"They didn't do it on purpose. Nobody got killed. Besides, they are planning to get married. That will be punishment enough."

As Coyle walked out of the office, he noticed O'Mally spin in his new chair as if in celebration.

Coyle headed down Bennett Avenue and checked his list to see who his next potential witness would be. He looked over his shoulder and wondered if O'Mally was still spinning in his new toy.

Bang, bang, bang.

It sounded like the town's fire alarm. *Another fire?* Coyle wondered. Had the fire restarted from embers? There was a fairly strong wind that day.

"The Portland Hotel," a passerby shouted.

Bang, bang, bang. A second alarm.

Instinctively, Coyle ran toward Second and Myers Avenue. The Portland was a ramshackle old building that went up as one of the first businesses in Cripple Creek. It had somehow been spared during the first fire. The roar of the flames made such a loud noise that they could be heard all across the Cripple Creek Mining District.

In a half hour the roof collapsed. That in turn caused the Portland's large broilers to explode. The explosion and the boiling water seriously injured six fire fighters. The falling roof sent a flood of hot embers skyward, and the brisk wind carried them to all corners of the business district and beyond.

Hungry flames licked the walls of hastily built, but now shabby, business buildings. Coyle stood in awe and watched yet another section of town go up in smoke. Shortly after the Portland fell, there was a tremendous rumble and boom as the Harder Grocery fire set off seven hundred pounds of dynamite. Disasters were going on around him so fast that Coyle did not know which way to turn.

N.O. Johnson's Clothing Store was built in brick like Johnson's main store in Colorado Springs. The Cripple Creek store was the only store still standing in its block on Bennett Avenue. Other stores and businesses were a few half-burned timbers standing in piles of charcoal and ash.

Amid the confusion Coyle heard "The fire has spread to the houses. Firemen are dynamiting houses to stop the spread." Sarah and Onie were in the house on Golden Avenue, and Coyle dashed up a hill to his temporary home.

"Sarah, is Onie alright? We have to get out of here."

"Andrew, thank God you're here. I didn't know where to go."

Just then a large man with black smears from charcoal on his face plunged through the door into the parlor. He had four sticks of dynamite in his hands.

"Get out. You are not going to dynamite this house," Coyle shouted.

"Who are you? Do you want to go up with the house?" the man with the dynamite snarled.

"This house belongs to the Woodward brothers, and they won't take kindly to anybody blowing it up. The wind is blowing the other way. There is no fire up here."

The big man froze.

"Get your big carcass out of our home. Go help somebody who needs it," Sarah scolded, pointing to the door.

Coyle said, "I remember you. You were knocked down at the train station explosion and I helped you get to a man with a horse and wagon to go to the hospital."

Sarah, unnoticed, had taken an antique shotgun with a broken stock off its rack on the wall. "Get out! We helped you then, but now I'll shoot you dead if you don't leave, *pronto*!"

Once they saw the dynamite-man going down the block, they prepared to leave. Coyle picked up Onie and Sarah grabbed a suitcase she had quickly packed when the fire started to spread.

"We don't need that. It will be too much to keep track of. Most people are gathering at the pond at Freeman's place," Coyle said.

"You take care of Onie and I'll take care of the suitcase," Sarah said through clinched teeth.

Sarah, with her suitcase, and Andrew, with Onie covered with a blanket to protect her from the flying debris and sparks, arrived at the pond and joined thousands of other Cripple Creek residents. Many had all their personal processions loaded into wheelbarrows, wagons, and even baby carriages.

At the altitude of Cripple Creek, the early spring nights were cold, so the crowd, wrapped in blankets and coats, at the pond huddled together and watched the glow just over the hill where the town was located. Eventually, the wind slowed down almost to calm. The crowd was almost warm.

CHAPTER 11

With mixed feelings and some confusion, Coyle got up to face the day. He felt refreshed and happy to have spent the night in his own bed with his family nearby after going sleepless at the pond, but there was a creepy feeling as he walked downtown. At Rosenthal's office, he saw charcoal and ash where thriving businesses had stood a couple of days ago.

"Good morning, Bart. It looks like you slept here in your office, or should I call you Mister Rosenthal?"

"You can call me mister tired-as-hell," Rosenthal chided.

"You look like it," Coyle said teasingly. "You look like you did after you spent over-nighters in college, and I don't mean cramming for a test the next day."

"These three days since the first fire make me feel like closing shop and walking away. At least half of the buildings are at least partially burned, and there are people with no homes. What else is there to do here? I just want to give up."

"What do you have against people, Bart?"

"Do you know how much they eat? It all started when my partner and I and a couple of mine owners met with Winston Sullivan in

Colorado Springs. It was a friendly enough meeting until Sullivan got the call. Mayor Romabelli said there were about five thousand people without food or shelter because of the fire."

"We made it to the pond at close to two or two-thirty," Coyle said. "But even in the middle of the afternoon the smoke blocked out the sun. I couldn't see, but I had no idea there were that many people there."

Rosenthal continued. "Well, that's what the mayor said. When he hung up Sullivan shouted, 'We've got to move and move fast. We can't take time to get pledges. Charge everything to me. We will divide the bills afterwards.' I don't suppose he is really counting on everybody paying."

"Paying for everything?" Coyle asked.

"We formed a relief committee. Sullivan was the chairman. He went to the Midland depot and ordered a two-car special train. Fred Woodward ordered twelve freight wagons and sent them to Shields Wholesale Grocery. I coordinated the volunteers who loaded canned beef and canned milk and cases and cases of beans, and crackers, and bread. You know volunteers, I had to load as much in the wagons as they did,"

Rosenthal was exhausted with emotion and had to sit.

"Harry Woodward called three different outfitting stores and cleaned them out of blankets and eight-person tents. O'Brian located a large tabernacle tent. And last but not least, Sullivan sent almost eight hundred diapers. You wouldn't think that old bachelor would have thought of diapers."

With a smile Rosenthal added, "I don't think I left out anything."

"You didn't see the two thousand people waiting at Midland Terminal cheering when the train came in," Coyle said. "Did you know Father Volson had all the pews moved to one side at St. Peter's Church, and that the sanctuary was reserved for mothers and babies?"

"We stayed at the pond all night because we didn't know if it would be safe to go home. Sarah had chased off one dynamiter the afternoon before. He looked drunk, and big. Big and drunk and dynamite don't mix. We definitely appreciated the things you sent up from the Springs."

Rosenthal said, "Take the day off and I will straighten up a few things here."

On his way out the door Coyle saw Rosenthal curl up on the office sofa.

Within a couple of weeks many of the new buildings were at least started, and almost all of them were brick. The Cripple Creek State Bank had set up operations in an empty warehouse to get the rebuilding started. *The Cripple Creek Times* moved and set up in a job press shop and didn't miss an issue. An investigation by Sheriff O'Mally revealed that the last round of fires was also an accident. It started when a kitchen worker spilled a pot of hot grease.

The star of downtown Cripple Creek was the National Hotel, which had been started before the fires and was the first building finished afterward. The National sat on the corner of 4th and Bennett. It was almost immediately known as the Brown Palace of Cripple Creek. There were telephones installed on all four floors. The National also introduced the first elevator in Cripple, and it ran twenty-four hours a day. Some of the rooms were classified as suites and had private baths.

Winston Sullivan signed a fifty-year lease for one of the National's most luxurious apartments. Sullivan apparently was showing his confidence in the mining district's future. With Sullivan's endorsement, townspeople no longer considered the National Hotel as somebody's daydream.

Coyle and Sarah agreed that they wanted to see the inside of the Brown Palace of Cripple Creek. Sarah was disappointed when they didn't get an invitation to attend the formal banquet to celebrate the grand opening. She was mollified, however, when Coyle told her just the uppity ups were invited to the banquet, but the entire town was invited to come and look around, and that's what they would do.

The night of the grand opening, Sarah broke the news that Katie from next door was going with them and John was going to sit with Meg and Onie.

"That would be nice, but wouldn't John want to go, too?" Coyle asked Sarah.

"John doesn't want to associate with the nose-up-in-the-air crowd, as he calls them. He told Katie someone who can afford what the National is charging would be better served renting a room at the Antlers in the Springs, a real classy hotel."

"John told Katie that the National would go broke in two years," Sarah continued. "Besides, a big crowd like that is no place for an almost four-year-old."

When they stopped to pick up Katie, Coyle noticed she was wearing one of Sarah's dresses. The women had been planning this all along. He saw there was no time to argue about it now.

The National did not disappoint. The furnishings were magnificent, and the artwork featured photos of Cripple Creek pioneers, many of whom were in attendance, and the elevator actually worked.

Sarah and Katie peeked in on the dining room. Katie pointed out many of the district's elite: the Woodward brothers, Maurice Finn, the lawyer for Winston Sullivan, Dr. Frank Hassenburg, Bert Carson.

"Bert Carson, doesn't he own most of the freight wagons in town?"

"Yes, and the bank, and some people say he will own most of Cripple District by the time he is done," Katie said.

She commented on whom she had just seen. "See that pretty, young lady with William Hurst? She is from the Springs and will be a stenographer for Mister Hurst, but she won't be for very long if Bert Carson has his way. Oh, look he is coming over to her now; some gals have all the luck."

Three hotel employees entered the dining room, one with a roast duck, and the other two with a roast pig. The waiters placed their well-laden trays in front of an ice sculpture of a swan. After appropriate "Ooooos" and "Ahaaas" Katie said, "Some gals have all the luck."

Sarah looked back and saw Coyle mentally twiddling his thumbs.

"Let's go upstairs. I hear Sullivan's suite is amazing." Sarah herded her little group toward the elevator.

"It is absolutely unbelievable," Sarah said upon stepping into the private room of the richest man in the district. "It looks like he has never slept in that big bed," Sarah said.

"No, he spends a lot of time in Colorado Springs. Gossip says he will probably buy a house down there some day. That is, if he can find some place where people won't bother him," Coyle said.

"Look at those mirrors. There must be ten or twelve of them around the room." Sarah looked to see if her petticoat showed.

"Surely you know what those are for?" Katie questioned.

Smirking, Coyle gently shook his head as a *no* sign in Katie's direction.

Katie changed the subject. "Look he has his own telephone. I wonder what his number is?" She laughed. "I might want to call him sometime."

The little group headed toward the elevator, but Sarah had said on ride up that the elevator made her nervous, so they walked down the four flights of stairs.

On the ground floor, they noticed a crowd gathering around the door to the barroom. With more than a little pushing and "Excuse me, excuse me," the three worked their way through the crowd to one corner of the bar.

They were just in time to see Barton Rosenthal ride his gray mare through the outside barroom door. "Yippio," Rosenthal hollered and held up two fingers indicating he was ordering two beers.

"Who is that riding behind him?" asked Sarah.

"Suellen Miller," Coyle answered. "I doubt that this shenanigan is the reason the judge allowed her to get out of jail on bail. But in Cripple Creek apparently anything goes."

Among the crowd, there were general whispers of, "Somebody is going to get stomped."

CHAPTER 12

"Good morning, Bart. Did you stop by the hotel last night to buy your horse a drink?"

"At the National? I didn't think Suellen would go along with it, but she did, and I couldn't let her bluff me out. We had a lot of fun. She is a good sport," Rosenthal said.

"She is also accused of murder and shouldn't be carrying on in public like that," Coyle scolded.

"You always were a spoilsport, Andrew. We never had any fun when you were around. I'll talk to Suellen about that. I already rented her a room in a house that wasn't burned, which isn't easy to find. There are lots of people looking for a place to stay. Sullivan only got a hundred and eighty-nine, eight-person tents. We are getting maybe a thousand more tents from Denver."

"You've been busy the last few days," Coyle said.

"How about you? Can you make a case that Suellen's innocent?"

"What can you tell me about Harry Woodward that I didn't get out of his brother Fred?"

Rosenthal took a few minutes to cogitate. "It is hard to think of the Woodwards separately because they do most big things together.

When they graduated from some Baptist college, their father gave each a thousand dollars. I guess most fathers do that. My father did, gave each of the five of us a thousand as a start. Anyway, the Woodwards bought McKinnie's placer mine. They planned to run cattle on the one hundred and thirty-six acres. But people wanted to build houses there, so the Woodwards laid out a town and named it Victor after one of the pioneers in the district."

Rosenthal paused as Coyle took notes. "The Woodwards started selling lots in Victor at an unexpected rate. Their sales were helped by the Woodwards' claim that there was gold under each lot."

Coyle looked up from his notes and smiled. "That's what you call good marketing."

"Good enough that the sale of building lots convinced Harry that he needed to build a hotel. They had just started to level the land for the Victor Hotel, when Harry found a small vein of gold. It looked promising enough that Harry followed the vein to the Gold Coin Mine, which the Woodwards bought for a few thousand dollars. Within a few months the miners followed the vein, and the Woodward boys owned a mine that was producing fifty thousand dollars in gold a month."

Coyle dropped his pencil.

Rosenthal said, "The rest you can ask about when you talk to Harry."

"Hello Harry. I'm Andrew Coyle, the lawyer representing Suellen Miller. I've talked to your brother, and I hoped to get your side of the story." Coyle was slightly surprised that Harry was much taller than his brother, Fred.

"There is no side to the story. The truth is the truth. No side to that. I've talked to Fred and everything he told you was true for me, too. I hope this won't take long. I am very busy."

Coyle continued. "I understand the entrance to your mine, I believe it's the Gold Coin, has the most beautiful shaft house anyone has ever seen. Brick walls, and colored windows. Must be impressive." Coyle found a chair and took a seat.

"Yah, we had the first Sunday school held in the district right there in the shaft house."

"What was the attendance?"

"Five, not counting me and Fred. Four woman and one man. Two of the women were our wives. Since then, we've reached ten a few times. You are invited if you are interested in Sunday school."

"I'll think about it. Right now, I am busy trying to learn about what happened at Opal DuPaulette's New Year's Eve party."

"Fred and I were not invited. Neither of us believes in dancing anyway. Our wives have given up asking about that. So, there wouldn't be any reason we would want to be there."

"French champagne and caviar?" Coyle countered.

"We have made enough money to buy French sparkling water if we drank, which we don't."

"What about Mister McKinnie? Was he upset that you only paid a few thousand dollars for the Gold Coin because you knew there was a vein that ran through his claim?"

"He was happy to get thousands for a mine that he thought was producing a piddling little bit. McKinnie thought he was getting the best of the deal. Do unto others what they are trying to do to you."

Coyle thanked Harry for his time and parted. He wondered what else the Woodward brothers could do with the fifty thousand a month the Gold Coin was producing.

Coyle got home and was visibly excited. He hugged Sarah and held Onie high over his head the way she liked it. Onie squealed and giggled. Although it was a rented house and the lease was up when the murder trial ended, Coyle felt strangely at home when there with his family.

Sarah sat quietly waiting for the big news. She had been married long enough to Andrew to decipher his moods. She knew Coyle had some good news.

"You know how the governor sent the state militia to keep the peace between the striking miners and the mine owners?" Coyle started.

"Yes, those soldiers leered at every woman on the street like we were one of the wretched ones. Even when Onie was with me."

Onie smiled at hearing her name, trying to interrupt, but her mother shushed her.

"When they got here everything was peaceful," Coyle said. "Tense, but peaceful. After a few days, the general requested permission to withdraw. The governor gave permission and the militia pulled out last night. Everybody was happy about that."

"I don't know which was worse, the union miner strikers or fighter substitutes or the soldiers hanging around," Sarah said with a sigh.

"This afternoon the union leader, Calderrock, found me in Rosenthal's office and offered me a job. I am to be the arbitrator at meetings between the union and the owners. Rosenthal said it was okay while we wait for the DuPaulette murder trial to come up on the docket."

"Oh Andrew," Sarah said as she hugged Coyle, "A judge."

"Not a real judge. Just an arbitrator. I make sure the talks are civil and I don't get to make the decision. I help the parties to agree on a decision. But I do make three dollars a day like a miner does and an extra dollar if the talks go over eight hours."

Coyle was greeted by a pair of small, outstretched arms.

"Daddy, swing me."

"Be careful in the house. That is outside playing you're talking about. Onie doesn't know any better, but you do, Andrew," Sarah admonished. "I have two children, not one."

———◆———

Coyle dashed into the meeting room, a spare room at the National Hotel. It was the only spare room in town. Management had brought in a temporary table with legs that folded up. Three men sat at each side. At the end Coyle saw an empty chair, which was slightly larger and padded.

"For me?" Coyle laughed, slightly embarrassed.

I don't want them to think I expect to be treated like a king, Coyle thought. Coyle looked at six stoic faces. He thought of a little story about why he was almost late hoping to soften the contentious mood.

"My daughter, Onie, spilled her milk. I saw it going and made a dive for the glass but was too late. Milk was all over. But worse yet, I knocked over the chair and the box sitting on it that we used to make it like a highchair. And of course, Onie fell off and was covered with milk, and crying. That's when my wife, Sarah, came out of the kitchen. And I don't have to tell you what she had to say."

"Come to the point. Your rent is up when the Opal DuPaulette trial is over, not when you finish the comedy hour," Rosenthal huffed.

"You are the chairman's landlord. How impartial is that?" Calderrock yelled.

Then six different voices harmonized in a chorus of dissatisfaction. None had permission to speak.

Coyle grabbed a convenient whiskey shot glass and used it to pound on the table three times. He raised his hand a fourth time when the room became silent. Coyle looked around at the stony faces. And then he looked at the substitute mallet in his hand. It was only then that he broke out in a cheery smile.

"I only want to get your attention and have some quiet. I didn't mean for that to sound like a fire alarm."

There were a couple of muffled chuckles. Other than that, the group stayed silent until—

"Let's introduce ourselves around the table. I'm Andrew Coyle, the attorney representing Suellen Miller accused of murder. And on my left, each one of you introduce yourself and tell us your occupation."

He pointed at Rosenthal.

Before Rosenthal could speak, Calderrock jumped up and bellowed, "How come they get to go first?"

Another voice came from the end of the table. "You like them best." So it went until noon.

The union men objected to everything the mine owners said. The mine owners seemed determined to give as good as they got. They sparred until someone said he had work to do, and Coyle told them the next meeting would start the next day at the same time.

CHAPTER 13

"Good morning, Sarah. I made a fire in the stove and warmed up some coffee."

"Aren't you going to have breakfast? Don't you know how much eggs cost? Thirty-six cents a dozen. In the Springs they are only a quarter."

"I'm going to the labor committee meeting. I don't want to be late again. Give Onie a kiss and tell her I'll be home for supper. And tell her not to spill her milk. Remember yesterday? That was a real mess." On his way out the door, Coyle stopped and added, "Speaking of a mess, that labor committee meeting is really a mess."

Sarah smiled and said, "Remember how you mopped up the milk yesterday? Go to your meeting and start mopping."

Coyle walked out into the sun and observed the workers and buildings resulting from their apparent hustle, bustle, and confusion. The brick buildings looked like a phoenix emerging from the ashes of two fires in a week. Cripple Creek was coming back. Stores, although far and few between, made Bennett Avenue a place to shop again. Many houses were livable again, a huge relief to those who had been residing in tents.

"Good morning Mister Coyle. I'm A.J. Tully, Barton Rosenthal's partner. I'll be sitting in for Bart today."

Coyle's mouth dropped open with surprise. In seconds, he pulled himself together and nonchalantly said, "You are the man on the train when the terminal annex was dynamited. You led us and the other passenger to safety and started helping the people on the station platform who were hurt in the explosion."

"Yes, I remember you. You make my actions sound more heroic than they actually were. Your wife and you did a lot of good first aid. Your wife is a real trooper."

"I guess we all did what we could," Coyle agreed.

"Oh, by the way, here is your belt she used for a tourniquet on the man who lost his leg, and your coat she gave him to keep him warm. She is a real trooper if there ever was one."

Coyle noticed that the topcoat had been cleaned and the blood stain barely showed. The morning had been frosty cold, and he was glad to get the coat.

"Thank you, Mister Tully. I'm glad to see you again, although this meeting is barely a better circumstance than the first time we met. By the way, why were you on the train from Denver?"

"Business."

"Just asking because you and Rosenthal seem to have plenty to keep you busy in the district."

"Quit your gabbing and let's get this meeting started," came the loudest voice from in the meeting room while other grumbles joined in.

Coye directed Tully to Rosenthal's seat and looked around for his shot glass that had been a perfect noise maker the day before. He was pleasantly surprised to see that someone had supplied him with a wooden mallet at his place at the table.

Bam, bam, bam! "Let's have some order here. Everybody in the seat you were sitting in yesterday, so I can remember your names. Names, and occupations, where you work. On my left, A.J. Tully, sitting in for Barton Rosenthal, partners in the Colorado Reduction and Mill. On my right side is Mike Calderrock, president of Western Miners Union."

So, he went down the table, alternating left side and right side making sure no one would accuse him of favoritism. "Harry Woodward, with his brother, owner of the Gold Coin; Marvin Goodson, acting mine superintendent at the Independence Mine; Winston Sullivan, prospector; and Brian O'Shay, engineer of the Dinky Train at the Apex mine."

"That was very good. Now if we can just keep some order we can arrive at a wage and hours settlement that nobody likes, but everybody likes some part of. Agreed?"

No response.

With everybody happy with their names and places at the table, Coyle felt like they had made progress. Next, he gave them rules he thought would keep the meeting civilized, or at least orderly.

"First, keep your comments limited to hours and wages. Second, we will alternate labor and management. Third, raise your hands for permission to speak. Fourth, no cussing and no derogatory comments about suggestions the other side has proposed."

Brian O'Shay spoke out loudly before Coyle was finished setting the rules. "I proposed to my wife and that got me into a whole shitload of trouble. And I don't want to marry any damn manager what wants to cut my stinking rate of pay. And what the hell does *der-hog-a-story* mean?"

The hours passed quickly, and Coyle and his mallet were worn out. The room went silent when a hotel employee came in with a pitcher of fresh water. He looked up and down the table and said, "No blood?" and scampered out of the room.

It was well past lunch hour, and the comments were coming louder and more heated. Coyle suggested that each mine should make their own agreement with the union rep at that mine. Those who needed miners more would have to pay more. All employees would have to be Miner's Union members, and if no union members were available, scabs could be hired if they joined the union. It sounded like something Coyle learned at the university. All the committee members were hungry and confident they could get the best deal at their particular mine by negotiating separately. So, the meeting broke up with nothing actually accomplished.

Coyle learned later that the committee members and two other mine owners met in a hotel room and agreed to stick together and pay two dollars and fifty cents for an eight-hour day. The Miner's Union met and made plans to break into the gunsmith's shop to steal as many guns as they could.

———•———

Coyle stopped home to tell Sarah that he was going to run down to Colorado Springs to check on Leon Redd, the mine superintendent who had been shot in an ambush while Coyle was at Winston Sullivan's Independence Mine. Coyle explained that if he had not been there, maybe the ambush would not have happened; he felt responsible that Redd had gotten shot.

Sarah waited patiently until Coyle took a breath and said, "I would like to go, too. I'm getting tired of potatoes and chipped beef and oatmeal for breakfast. Katie next door said she would show me how to cook something different for a change. She said anybody can cook if they have a can opener. We don't have a can opener in this house."

"Well, I'm going to the hospital, and I don't want you to have to wait around. I don't know how long I might be there."

"That's okay. I'll meet you at Best Food, that store next to the hat shop. Leona, get your coat. We are going with Daddy on a train ride."

Coyle was surprised that Onie stayed out of sight behind the one big easy chair in the parlor. Sarah went to retrieve their daughter and put Onie on her lap.

"I don't wanna to go on the train," Onie sobbed.

"Why not?" Sarah questioned.

"When we went on the train before, the big boom made lots of people be dead. I don't want you and Daddy to be dead."

"We will be real careful and take care of you, and we will all have a good time. Is that right, Daddy?"

"We don't want to miss the train," Coyle said.

With a forced laugh, Sarah said, "Okay, let's have a fun train ride."

CHAPTER 14

"Hello, Mister Redd. May I call you Leon?"
"Sure, Mister Coyle. Good to see you."
"Andrew."
"Andrew, they told me, you saved my life. Thank you."

Coyle glanced around the hospital room. There were three other beds. Just one was occupied by a blacksmith who was kicked by a horse and broke his knee.

"How are you feeling?" Coyle returned his gaze back to Redd.

"I can't move without pain. They couldn't get the bullet out. It was too close to some organ or other. How are things going at the mine?" Redd couldn't help thinking about the Independence gold mine where he had been the superintendent, but which he would probably never see again.

"I haven't been to the mine again since the day of the ambush, but I've been meeting with a committee of management and union representatives. Mister Sullivan is on the committee. He said the nonunion miners are doing fine. He is having trouble replacing you. A mine super with experience doesn't grow on trees, you know."

They both sat quiet for a bit, cogitating. Coyle broke the silence with a remark that sounded like it had just occurred to him but actually it was the reason he wanted to visit Redd.

"Do you have any idea who would want to kill you? Can you guess who the guy was?"

"He was small and moved like a woman. Wasn't no guy. I bet it was a gal."

Just then a nurse came in with Redd's supper tray. Redd said, "They feed us early so we can go to sleep early. Once we are asleep, they come in to take our pulses and check our blood pressure and whatever to make sure we don't get any sleep."

"Amen," the blacksmith joined in.

"You will have to go now, Mister Coyle," said the nurse in her crisp white uniform and nurse's hat. "We are quite busy at this time."

As Coyle put on his topcoat to leave, he whispered, "How is the food here?"

Redd looked up at the no-nonsense nurse standing at the foot of his bed and then back at Coyle. "On time," he said.

"Visiting time is over," the nurse said, and she was tapping her toe.

———•———

Coyle stopped at the store that Sarah had described as a "cute little hat shop." He assumed she would go there after grocery shopping. At the door, he looked around. All he saw was two woman exchanging hats to try them on for looks, and a bored salesclerk daydreaming. He looked around, but no Sarah. The two customers saw him, giggled, and promptly returned the hats and the clerk gratefully gathered up the merchandise. When he saw the two women reaching for their pocketbooks and getting ready to leave, he touched his hat in a gesture of politeness. He ducked out the door and headed to Best Foods.

The first thing he saw in the grocery was Onie looking at the candy display case. There were four more shelves of food items and a meat case. The butcher was busy explaining to Sarah the difference between a steak and a pot roast.

She saw Coyle and turned back to the butcher and said, "We'll take them both." She turned to Coyle and said, "Isn't this wonderful, clams in a can and all these vegetables in cans."

At the cash register, Coyle saw half a dozen cans, a bunch of carrots, and the two packages of meat neatly tied in butcher paper.

Coyle added, "A can opener and a peppermint stick for Onie."

The clerk offered to have the order delivered to Cripple Creek District by a boy for four-bits carrying charges. Sarah noticed the clerk's eyes sizing up her fashionable blue dress and slender figure.

"Oh no," Sarah protested, "my husband can handle it."

"I can carry it if you can cook it," Coyle replied as he picked up the cardboard box with some reservations.

"Don't drop it. Why do you think I brought you along?" Sarah conveniently forgot who was accompanying whom.

As they approached the house, Coyle marveled that he had never noticed how far it was from terminal annex train station to home. He asked Sarah to take the key out of his coat pocket while he held on to the box of groceries. Sarah immediately noticed a message tacked to the door.

Sarah put her hand over her mouth to stifle her scream. Onie startled and froze.

Coyle stepped in to see what was wrong. He read the note and almost dropped the box of groceries.

Get out of town or there will be another fire and your family will be in it.

"Open the door," Coyle demanded. "The key is in my coat pocket."

"Is my pepper stick in your pocket, Daddy?"

"You be a good girl and I'll tell you where you can find the peppermint stick. Later but not now. We are busy now."

"Where is the key? Your damned coat has so many pockets," Sarah huffed.

CHAPTER 15

When the three Coyles walked into his office, Rosenthal was waiting for them.

"Here's the note." Coyle held out the crumbled piece of paper threatening them. "I need to withdraw from the case and get my family out of here."

After a careful reading Rosenthal said, "You can't drop the case. We need you. Suellen Miller needs you. As for your family, hello Sarah, and hello Leona, they can stay in Colorado Springs with my friend Julia and her parents. The Lewis' have a big house right on Bijou Street and there will be plenty of room for you, Sarah, and Onie, too. You will be safe there. I'll be seeing Julia tonight and make all the arrangements for you."

"We don't want to stay in Colorado Springs, and we don't want Andrew to take the case." Sarah was emphatic.

Rosenthal's big smile and pleading eyes that had worked to persuade his friend so often in the past had no effect.

"You know you're a Harvard man and we know Harvard men don't give up that easily. Besides there is a handsome fee involved. And we know Harvard men don't—" Rosenthal paused and took a deep breath. "Never mind, we will keep you safe. We must win this case, and there is no time to start over again with new representation."

On their way back to the rental house Coyle said, "The Lewis family is reputed to be very nice. Colorado Springs is more like a city than a gold camp. You will like that."

Sarah smiled solemnly. "I can go back to Denver and stay with my family. They are reputed to be nice people. You can stay in Cripple Creek and play games with your old college chum the Harvard man."

Coyle's red mustache quivered as he tried to suppress his frustration. "You know your uncle and his new wife moved into your room above the haberdashery. So, where are you going to live in Denver? Honestly Sarah, I don't appreciate your sarcasm."

Onie tugged on Coyle's coattail. "Daddy, will my peppermint stick be sour?"

Sarah shushed her daughter and said to Coyle, "You'll promise to come see me when court is not in session?'

At that moment they heard something behind them. They turned around and saw a fire wagon sweep by on Golden Avenue.

Coyle dropped the box of groceries and grabbed a resisting Onie and put her against his chest. "Come on, let's go!" he said gesturing with his head. "It might be John and Katie's house."

They ran past one of the only blocks in Cripple Creek that had not been touched by one of the two previous fires. There was a crowd and a bucket line putting water on the hungry flames.

"Oh no, it's—" She couldn't get the words out.

Coyle put Onie down and put her hand on Sarah's dress. "Stay with Mama. Hold on tight." With that, he pushed through the crowd of onlookers and jumped up on the front porch. He touched the doorknob, but the heat was too much. Coyle used the coat tail of his frock coat to get a good grip and jerked the door open. The flames responded with a huge whoosh blasting through the doorway. Coyle fell backward and then scurried down the steps.

"Are you okay? I don't want you to be a hero," Sarah called out. "Get back over here. I just want you to be safe."

"I'm fit as a fiddle, but I can't say that for the house." Coyle tried to smile.

Sarah said between tears, "Everything we owned was in that house." As they watched in horror, Sarah whispered in Coyle's ear, "Do you think it was the person who left the note?"

"Do you think it wasn't? I'm more determined than ever to get to the bottom of this."

The roof caved in, and the parlor window exploded sending glass over the crew of firefighters. Coyle looked at the bystanders one by one. He had learned that the criminal often shows up at the scene of the crime just to revel in what he has done and watch the victims suffer. However, none of the gawkers looked suspicious to Coyle, and there was no one present who he knew.

"I hope the houses on either side are safe. I'll tell the firemen to put some water on our neighbors' houses to save them and stop the fire from spreading," Coyle said.

"Doesn't the fire make you change your mind? The fire means that note is telling you what is going to happen," Sarah said, her voice quivering from fear and anger. She was finally saying how she really felt, and Coyle could tell from her tone she did not like the life in a gold camp, not even a prosperous one like Cripple Creek.

"No, if I leave the district now it will mean they won. And Opal DuPaulette's killer will be free to kill again. I don't want that to happen," Coyle said.

Sarah finally noticed what Coyle was unaware of; his eyebrows and his precious red mustache were singed. She had forgotten about Onie, who was still clinging to her skirt. "You can tell Onie to let go now," she said to her husband.

Coyle gave Sarah a kiss on the cheek and told her to stay where he could find her. She was unresponsive until Onie hugged her mother's leg in fear. Sarah grabbed her hand and started nervously pacing, trying to compose herself and figure out what next to do.

She didn't like to be told what to do, but she had to find a safe place to stay, a place where Coyle could find her. *What else can I do? I am only a woman. I hope Onie has more choices when she is grown than I have had.* Sarah lamented.

Coyle returned from the backyard and Sarah stopped pacing and ran into her husband's arms. Onie was close behind and grabbed Coyle's leg.

"Are you alright? I was worried about you," Coyle asked. No answer above the sobs. "The firemen turned their hoses onto John and Katie's house. A wet house should not burn, or at least not as easily as this one did."

"I never liked that old house anyway," Sarah said. "But I love you a lot. Please don't ever leave me again." Sarah sobbed.

CHAPTER 16

After a quiet night in the Imperial Hotel and breakfast at Joe's Café, Sarah and Onie were ready to go with Coyle to Rosenthal's office to learn what arrangements he had made for their housing. Onie still was squeamish about a train ride, but excited to be venturing to a new place.

They waited for close to half an hour, but no Rosenthal. Just as they were gathering up their things to leave, the office door opened with a bang and Rosenthal burst in.

"Sorry I'm late. I've been talking to Harry Woodward. He's a little steamed up over the house, but I tried to tell him it wasn't your fault, that some arsonist likely torched the place to scare you off."

Rosenthal paused for a second and looked Coyle in the eye. "It wasn't your fault, was it?"

"No Bart, it wasn't our fault. We weren't home when the blaze started. We were here with you, remember?"

Rosenthal shrugged. "Anyway, Harry doesn't have any other vacant houses to rent for you, so we'll have to figure that out. But Sarah is all set. The Lewis family in Colorado Springs is happy to see her and your little girl." Rosenthal waved at Onie while he continued.

"The trial starts tomorrow, Andrew. I don't think it would be practical to ride the train down to Colorado Springs and back twice a day. I've got a deal for you that you will like. Let's take Sarah and Leona to the train station and then show you your new home."

"You'll love the Springs. Here let me help you with your luggage."

Rosenthal palmed his forehead and said to Coyle, "Oh, I'm sorry, I forgot you lost everything in the fire." He turned to Sarah. "Julia loves shopping. She knows all the good places for bargains. You are going to be a good pair. Hurry, we don't want to miss the train."

The train station and loading platform had been largely repaired. Onie stared at the spot where Sarah had tried to help a victim, remembering the horrors of the day they arrived from Colorado Springs.

The train arrived on schedule from its trip around the mines of the Cripple Creek Mining District. Next stop would be Colorado Springs, and Coyle had a feeling that Sarah was going to like civilization for a change. The night shift workers from the upper limit mines unloaded from the train and then headed for home by way of their favorite saloon. Sarah held onto Onie with one hand and clutched the paper with the Lewises' address in her other hand. They got onto the train after the rush of off-passengers had departed.

Onie's smiling face appeared in the window first and then Sarah's smile appeared over the top of Onie's head. Coyle could not read lips well, but he was sure Sarah said, "I love you." Coyle threw her a kiss as the train pulled out of the station. He hated to see them go and felt uneasy about them traveling unescorted to a strange place, convincing himself that it was the right choice to remove them from harm's way.

Rosenthal was in a hurry to leave the station and Coyle had no time to further console himself. As they walked the few blocks to the business area of Bennett Avenue, Rosenthal kept up a constant line of chatter about the good deal Coyle was getting for accommodations during the time the trial was going on. Rosenthal confided that he didn't think the trial would take that long because Suellen was clearly innocent, at least innocent of having killed Opal DuPaulette.

Rosenthal led Coyle into the business section of Bennett Avenue. Coyle was admiring what a nice day it was. Winter changing to spring, and no one knew what the weather would be like in a couple of hours. Coyle was having a hard time keeping up with Rosenthal, slowing to look at the emerging new town. It was like a phoenix coming back to life after the fire. Suddenly Rosenthal stopped.

"Here we are," Rosenthal announced.

Coyle looked around. "The only building on this side of the street within half a block is the National Hotel."

"Right, you are my old buddy. Let's go in and see what we've got for you."

Coyle nodded an accepting smile to Rosenthal's invitation "to come on in."

"I'm surprised to see management will allow you to come again after that shenanigan with you, and the horse in the bar."

Rosenthal corrected Coyle. "You mean me, my horse and your client."

"I wouldn't mention that I am your old buddy, Bart, and I would appreciate it if you would not mention it to your friend either. Not until the trial is over." Coyle went through the main door being held open by Rosenthal.

Rosenthal countered with, "I trust you told Sarah not to mention that evening to Julia while she is staying with the Lewises?"

"You know how women talk." Deep inside his professional image a little part of Coyle was enjoying seeing Barton Rosenthal swallow the truth with a big gulp and a deep sigh.

Coyle glanced around the opulent lobby. The central chandelier was even grander than he remembered. The wine-colored draperies matched the upholstery in the room, and that is what Sarah and Katie had commented on the night of the grand opening. Of course, the cut flower bouquets were gone, but Coyle had not paid attention to them when he had accompanied the ladies. He probably would not have noticed them now either.

A short walk to the elevator and Coyle and Rosenthal were on their way up. "Four, please."

The uniformed operator answered, "Sorry sir, that is a private apartment. I can't take you there."

"Sorry," Rosenthal said. "But this has been cleared with Mister Sullivan. It is on the square. Mister Coyle here is going to occupy the penthouse for a few days. Now, take us up, please."

"Well Dandy Andy, what do you think of these digs?" Rosenthal teased.

"It is a bit nicer than the house that burned down."

"It is a whole lot nicer than where I am living. And I am rich." Rosenthal was all smiles.

"There are a lot of mirrors." Coyle was remembering the night he and Sarah and Katie first saw the room.

"Huge bed, or as I call it an adult playground."

Coyle was unmoved. "Barton, I know you must have pulled some strings to get Winston Sullivan to okay my staying in this room, his room. It is common knowledge that he does not intend to live here. The apartment and the whole hotel are just a come-on to get people to want to stay here. I appreciate your efforts, but I can't stay here. Mister Sullivan is a potential, albeit unwilling, witness in a murder trial that I am a part of. It might be construed as a bribe to influence me one way or another. The Imperial is good enough for me, and you are paying the bill. I'm doing you a favor by saying, 'No thanks.'"

"Someday," Rosenthal dreamed out loud, "when I am really rich, I will build a hotel the way I want it. My hotel will be in a European style. Of course, you will be invited."

"You are already rich. I can wait for you to get really rich. In the meantime, I will catch the noon train up to Money Mountain and explain to Sullivan why I am not living in his hotel room in the National. Maybe he will change his mind about appearing in court. I have a feeling he knows more about what is going on than what he is telling us," Coyle smiled, turned, and walked away.

CHAPTER 17

"Good afternoon, Mister Sullivan. I am Andrew Coyle."

"I remember you. I ain't that drunk. What do you want, Mister Lawyer?"

"First, I wanted to tell you that I am sorry that things didn't go well at the negotiations with the union and the management."

"You did the best you could." Sullivan stepped aside and motioned for Coyle to come in. Sullivan's white hair was tangled and spiked, but he was neatly dressed in his black suit with a vest and necktie. His inconsistent appearance matched his complex personality.

"Maybe if we got some different people on both sides, they would work together and get something accomplished," Coyle offered.

"Maybe if we got some different people together, they could jump over the moon," Sullivan chided and laughed until he started choking.

Coyle jumped up from the easy chair and started toward Sullivan who was bent over from the waist. Between coughs Sullivan waved Coyle away and pointed at a bottle of whiskey on the table.

Coyle retrieved the bottle and a drinking glass and handed it to Sullivan. Sullivan grabbed the bottle. After one long pull on the whiskey, the coughing stopped, and Sullivan stood up straight.

"You know how long I looked before I found this payload? Nigh on to forty years. I've been all over this state and some other places that are not even states yet. Nobody paid me. I earned every nickel of my grubstake building houses in the winter so in the summer me and my burro could traipse to every godforsaken corner that I thought might have something to mine. And mine we did. I always pulled my weight with a pick and shovel." Sullivan crossed the room and was sitting on a horsehair sofa. "These greenhorns want to get paid a ransom for digging what I found. They wouldn't know gold if they looked in a dentist's mouth."

"How did you come to find this claim?"

"Sit down and I'll tell you what nobody else knows. Here goes." Winston Sullivan began telling how he found the richest claim on Money Mountain.

"There was this Frenchman named Lamont Perlmon. He represented a San Francisco syndicate, and he didn't want to go back and tell them he didn't buy anything. I didn't like him very much. He kept pestering me about buying the Molly B True. He came to my cabin, this cabin, with another offer. To get rid of Perlmon, I offered to sell him the Independence on a thirty-day option. He asked me how much. I told him one hundred and fifty-five thousand. That was almost the highest price for a mine by two times up 'til then. I thought that would get him out of my hair. That bucko sat down and wrote a check. A thirty-day option at full price.

"I knew Perlmon and his crew would show up in the morning, so I went out to clear out my equipment and stuff. Got the mining gear stuff out of three crosscuts. I just about skipped the fourth crosscut. We gave up on it last year. I had been using that crosscut as a storage area for some junk and a few tools. One was a shovel with a broken handle.

"Old habits. I picked up the shovel and started scratching around at the loose gravel and found the kind of coloration gravel that indicates a vein."

"How come you did not see it before? Were you too late? Perlmon already had the option."

"It started the next morning. So, I put all the junk back and scattered some sand and rocks around so no one would suspect anybody had been diggin'. The little room looked like it hadn't been touched for a year."

"And you weren't about to tell them," Coyle chuckled.

"Hell, no, I wasn't going to tell them. If they were going to find anything it was because they did the looking. It was the longest thirty days of my life. Many a night I couldn't sleep. Finally, the night before the option was up, my good friend Perlmon and I went out to dinner. I liked him a lot better by then."

"After dinner, which he paid for, he lit a big cigar. He pulled out the agreement and said something about since he was leaving in the morning the paper wouldn't mean anything. So that son of a Frenchman held the contract up to the cigar and lit it. I jumped up and opened the door of the potbelly stove. He dropped the burning paper contract in the fire. God bless him."

"How much has the Independence produced so far?"

"Two thousand a day for a couple years now."

"How come if that is such a big secret, you told me?"

"Truth is, I wouldn't have all that money if I hadn't lied about the value of the mine I was offering Perlmon with an option to buy."

"Legally you didn't lie. It was more a lie of omission. Different judges interpret the intent of the omission and the circumstances. It probably won't come up unless it is somehow connected to Suellen Miller and her case."

"I don't want to take that chance," Sullivan sighed in relief of having told somebody his secret. "I don't want to lose the Independence. Not over some courtroom technicality."

Coyle removed his watch from his vest pocket home and checked the time. "I better be on my way." He gathered up his things and took a sideward glance at Sullivan. To Coyle, Sullivan looked forlorn, as if he had already lost the Independence to Perlmon.

Upon leaving, Coyle turned in the doorway and said, "See you in court. That's an old lawyer's saying. Might apply to you. Thanks again for offering your room in the National. And by the way, I will see you in court. I am afraid you're going to have to testify."

———•◆•———

It was an hour or more before the train made its rounds in the mining district and started its way back to Cripple Creek. Coyle thought he could make use of the time by stopping in on Jimmy O'Brian, who was the Mayor of Victor besides in addition to being the primary stockholder of the Frisco Lady Mine.

The Frisco was only a short walk down the hill from the Independence. Only it was not as short of a walk as Coyle remembered. He walked in the flat area next to the tracks, stepping over an occasional rock that had fallen down the hill and rested next to the rail. Other than that, it was smooth sailing and Coyle made good time because of the downhill slope of the path.

Coyle was admiring how blue the sky was and how sharp the spruce trees looked against the sky in the clear mountain air. The tracks made a sharp right turn and went over the hill. Coyle followed the tracks around the bend and saw a mine that he had seen on the way up. He didn't remember seeing so many saddle horses and so many wagons there before, or the large crowd of men gathered at Frisco Lady mine.

Most of the men glared ominously at him. There was no turning back, even though he was tempted. Coyle noticed that many of them held revolvers. Then he saw that Sheriff O'Mally was among them. Coyle thought, *It looks like a posse to me.*

CHAPTER 18

"You know who I am, Sheriff. We met when the union and management meeting got out of hand."

Sheriff O'Mally sat on the desk of the office shack of the Frisco Lady mine. One of his deputies leaned against the door, leaving the only chair in the shack for Andrew Coyle, who still stood handcuffed. The lawyer saw several members of what he determined to be the sheriff's posse taking turns peering in the window and snickering.

"I guess you know why I'm here and why you, Coyle, are under arrest."

"No, Sheriff, I have no idea what you are talking about."

"Winston Sullivan has been murdered and you were the last one to see him alive."

"Correction, Sheriff, the murderer was the last one to see him alive, and I didn't murder him. I don't even have a gun."

"How did you know Sullivan was shot? I just said he was murdered."

"Isn't that the common way to murder somebody in this country? Lot of people have a gun. Everyone has a gun to protect themselves from everyone else who has a gun."

"The posse will look for your gun. You must have tossed it somewhere between the Independence Mine and the Frisco. The miners at the Independence saw you walking away real fast down the railroad tracks instead of waiting for the train like you usually do. One miner went into Sullivan's house to see why the train stopped running and that is why you were walking. He found Sullivan dead."

"I was out rounding up a posse just when you showed right on time. You got anything to add to it?"

"I was coming to see Jimmy O'Brian and see if he knows anything about Opal DuPaulette's death. That's why I was meeting with Mister Sullivan. I'm saying that meeting was not murder. Did anyone see me do anything out of the ordinary or violent?"

"Jimmy O is out of town. You should have called him first," Sheriff O'Mally chided.

"Not everyone has a telephone," Coyle retorted. "Besides, I was enjoying the scenery."

"I think you will enjoy the scenery where you are going. Many, many iron bars. You can count them until your head swims."

"You can't do that. I'm due in court tomorrow."

"Remember me?" The sheriff took off his hat and flashed a clownish grin. "You put my name on the witness list. I'll be in court *with you* tomorrow. We can walk over to the courthouse together."

Coyle struggled a little to stand, his legs shaky. He had forgotten about the handcuffs on his wrists. "I'll be honored," he said sarcastically.

"Dusty, go bring the wagon around for Mister Andrew Coyle. Send half the posse to look for Coyle's gun. Both sides of the tracks, and all the way up to the Independence. Tell the other half of the posse to go with us to the jail in Cripple. Take names and tell them they'll get their fifty cents posse fee on the first of the month."

———◆———

At his office and jailhouse, O'Mally looked at an empty cell and nodded. "Your new home," he said to Coyle.

Coyle saw a telephone on the sheriff's desk. "May I call my wife and tell her where I am?"

"Okay, but make it quick. The lunchroom is going to call me to ask what I want for dinner." The sheriff patted his more than adequate belly. "Andy, they want to know how many prisoners we have. They already know what the prisoners get for their dinners. Just want to know how many guests we have."

A friendly voice came over the telephone. "Number please." Coyle gave the operator the number. Operator said, "That is long distance to Colorado Springs."

"I know it is long distance," Coyle answered. Sheriff O'Mally nearly dropped his coffee cup.

"No long-distance calls," the sheriff barked.

"Sheriff O'Mally is paying for it," Coyle said.

The friendly voice on the telephone said, "Tell Archie hello." Click.

Coyle turned to Sheriff O'Mally and said, "Hello, Archie." Coyle held one finger to his mouth indicating he needed silence. "It is long distance."

Sarah was summoned to the phone by the maid. She answered with a giddy chuckle. "Hello, Andrew, I've been waiting for you to call."

"Did you find the Lewis family okay? No problems?"

"No problems. Mister Lewis sent the butler to meet our train. No problems. The Lewis family is friendly. They are nice people," Sarah said.

"Well, there is one problem. Sheriff O'Mally thinks I killed Winston Sullivan. He arrested me and is locking me away in jail. Please call Barton Rosenthal and ask him to bail me out." Coyle could not believe Sarah's answer.

"I leave you for one day and you end up in jail! My father had a name for that. *Dumbkoff*."

"You know I didn't do it. I just have to prove I couldn't have done it. But that will take time."

"My sweet, sweet Dumbkoff. I'll come back to Cripple Creek and get you out of that place."

"No, you will be safer there. You need to take care of Leona. Call Barton and tell him I will explain everything after he gets me out of jail."

"No need. Barton is here visiting Julie. He will be glad to talk to you," Sarah whispered into the telephone. "Julie is pursuing him with great determination."

"Like you pursued me?"

"Dumbkoff."

"Tell Onie that I love her." Coyle waited.

In a matter of minutes Rosenthal called the sheriff's office demanding to speak with Coyle.

"I hear you are in jail. That is not quite the arrangements I would have picked for you, but as long as you are happy. At least you will not get in any trouble where you are."

"This is no time for joking around. You know damned well I'm not happy where I am," Coyle huffed. "Catch the first train here up here to Cripple and bail me out." Coyle looked up and saw Sheriff O'Mally striding back and forth and tapping his toe each time he turned around and started in the opposite direction.

Rosenthal chuckled over the phone. "First train out of the Springs is in the morning. See you then. By the way, Julie is taking Sarah shopping tomorrow. I assume the amount she spends will come out of your fee. Bye."

CHAPTER 19

Unshackled, Coyle, escorted by Rosenthal, walked across the street to the courthouse with Sheriff O'Mally about four steps behind. It was as if nothing out of the ordinary had happened, just a lawyer and the sheriff going to the court.

They met Suellen Miller sitting at the defendant's table drawing tiny pictures on one of the court-furnished yellow pads of paper. She looked very pretty in her dark blue dress buttoned up to her neck, and a white collar that reached her chin.

O'Mally took the audience seats just behind the defendant's table. Coyle walked through the gate of the little fence that separated the gallery from the trial floor. Rosenthal followed Coyle to the defendant's table. Coyle hesitated for a second and then decided Rosenthal was paying for the privilege. *Why have an argument now?*

As Coyle approached the defendant's table, Suellen smiled broadly and pulled out a chair for him.

A pretty smile, but a little too pretty for a defendant, a little too happy, Coyle thought.

The bailiff came to the front of the room and announced, "All rise." There was a general hubbub as the twenty or so spectators stood.

"The district court of the Fourth District, and Teller County, the Honorable Samuel Avon presiding."

Judge Avon said, "Be seated," and pounded once with his gavel. "The main order of business is to pick a jury. Is that what you are here for? If not, please stand." Four people rose, but one prospective juror was pulled down. The man next to him mumbled something like, "You can't get outa this that easy." Judge Avon continued by addressing the three men standing. "Get your butts out of here or I'll be calling for a jury to try your sorry bag of bones."

Suellen leaned over and behind her hand whispered, "Savanna Sam, he's a tough one."

"You know him?"

"He's from Georgia and still mad about losing the war," Suellen whispered.

"Mister Coyle." Judge Avon glared over the top of his gold rimmed glasses. "Do you have something to say before I describe the jury selection procedure?"

"No, Your Honor."

"Listen, and keep your pie hole shut," Avon continued without waiting for a reply from Coyle.

Coyle remembered picking a jury in Leadville when two prospective jury members were involved in a fist fight before serving. What a mess that was. He didn't know anything about these Cripple Creek men, but he had to select eight of them. The district attorney could refuse two of Coyle's choices, and Coyle could refuse two selections of the district attorney's eight choices. If one juror was selected by both parties, they had to negotiate who would be added to make a final total of twelve men.

As it turned out, the twelve seemed to be a good sample of the Cripple Creek population: four businessmen, four mine owners, four miners—two union and two nonunion. Two alternates were also selected. Gamblers, pimps, and government employees were weeded out. Coyle felt satisfied they had done a good day's work.

Sheriff O'Mally walked out of the courtroom with Coyle and Rosenthal. Coyle was surprised to see Sarah waiting in the hallway inside the main door. Coyle said to O'Mally, "Can you give me a minute to talk to my wife?"

"No hurry," the sheriff answered. Mister Rosenthal here paid to bail you out this morning. He also paid Miss Suellen Miller's bail yesterday to get her out of the women's jail. If you and Miss Miller don't show up, Mister Rosenthal is going to be out a lot of money, That's the way the bail system works. Good day."

Rosenthal waved on his way out. "Don't forget to show up," he laughed.

"I am glad to see you too," Coyle said as he gave Sarah a big hug. "Where is Onie?"

"She is with the Lewis family. Julie will make a good mother. I hope Barton Rosenthal knows that. Bart and I will take the afternoon train to the Springs. I hope you don't mind, but I have to buy some more clothes. Bart will pay for them out of your retainer."

"No, I don't mind," Coyle said, but his face said, *We aren't going to make any money on this case.*

"Oh, come on you big skinflint. You don't want your ladies walking around in dirty clothes while the women in the Old Homestead are sashaying about in the latest fashions."

As they walked together to the train station, Sarah was more interested in discussing the Lewis family and Julia's ambition to become part of Rosenthal's family than her husband's legal plight or the woman he was defending.

"She even sent a maid over to wash all the dirty dishes and clean the house at least a little bit," Sarah summed it up to a distracted Coyle.

Rosenthal was at the terminal waiting for the train to take him to Colorado Springs for his nightly visit with Julie. "Hi, Sarah, I was hoping I would have company on the ride to the Springs." Rosenthal turned to Coyle and with a laugh, "Don't worry, Andy, I will take good care of her."

Coyle replied, "Not to worry, she can take care of herself."

Once again Coyle felt a little downhearted seeing his wife going away while he was left standing alone. Sarah leaned out of the train window to blow him a kiss as the train pulled out.

Coyle answered with, "I'll telephone you each night after the trial."

The housing crunch for displaced residents in Cripple Creek had eased in the past weeks and Coyle felt confident of finding a room at the older and cheaper Imperial, which he had told Rosenthal and Sarah.

"Good afternoon, I would like to get a room for one. I might have to stay for a couple of weeks and would like to pay you when my date of departure is determined."

"Ain't no problem, sir. Arrangements have already been made by Mister Rosenthal. Here are your keys, Room 205. I'll get you a bell hop to help you with your luggage."

Coyle chuckled. "No luggage. I'll get a shave at the barber shop next door in the morning."

As Coyle walked away, the desk called out, "Good luck in court tomorrow."

Coyle was unphased. It seemed that in a town of ten thousand residents, at least half were aware of him as both the defender for a client accused of murder, and a person accused of murder. He stopped and raised a hand and smiled, then he started up the stairs to his room.

As he walked down the hall looking at room numbers a voice startled him. "If you are looking for 205, it is down here next to the bathroom."

Coyle looked up, startled. "Suellen, you surprised me. I didn't expect to see you here."

"My lawyer told me to stay away from the Old Homestead before the trial. It would give me a bad image."

"So, I did." Coyle was embarrassed "But I didn't expect to see you in this hotel."

"Had to economize. My fellow coworkers are stealing my business, and the hotel management doesn't allow my profession here. You had better get the trial finished fast so I can get back on my back." With a snicker she said, "I mean back on my feet."

Coyle looked back at his room number.

Suellen said, "It is convenient for you to be next to the bathroom. But it was convenient for everyone else on the second floor to open and close the bathroom door with a bang. And by the way, the door squeaks."

"How do you sleep?"

"Ear plugs. My room is 204. It is just as noisy as your room."

"That will work out nicely. We can walk to the courthouse together in the morning. That should change some people's image, yours, mine, or both."

Suellen turned with a swish that made her natural dishwater-blond hair fall over her shoulder and released the faint aroma of lilies.

Something about the woman aroused him.

Coyle watched her take the few steps to her room and enter. Then he heard the door shut with an unnecessarily loud slam. He remembered Sarah didn't use perfume. For some reason he almost forgot to call Sarah. Coyle immediately went looking for a telephone to call Colorado Springs.

CHAPTER 20

The morning was bright and sunny. *A good day to go to court,* Coyle thought. He hurried off to the barbershop to get a shave and then decided on a haircut, as well. Even his red mustache was trimmed above his upper lip. He not only looked good, and after a splash of aftershave, he smelled nice, too.

Suellen Miller was supposed to meet him in front of their hotel but was nowhere in sight. Coyle could understand why she did not want to stand on a street corner. She would likely get propositioned. He went inside the hotel and after a look around the lobby and adjoining bar, the idea hit him. *Just like a woman. Never ready on time.*

It was getting late, so Coyle took the stairs to the second floor. The elevator was too slow. Down the hall to room 204. Coyle knocked on the door a little too hard. The door opened a crack and Coyle saw a hotel maid with a broom in her hand.

"Hello, I'm Andrew Coyle from 205, I need to see Miss Miller. Is Miss Miller here?"

"No, sir. Went to court this mornin'. She'll be back this evening."

Coyle rushed down the steps two at a time. He crossed the lobby and reached the front door and sprinted up the Bennett Avenue hill.

At the door of the courtroom the bailiff had just finished saying the Honorable Samuel Avon presiding. Coyle slid into his chair at the defendant's table next to his client.

"Nice of you to join us, Mister Coyle." Before Coyle could answer, Avon added, "Don't ever be late to a trial that I am trying again."

"It won't happen—" Coyle was cut off by the sharp sound of a mallet on wood.

"You've made friends with the judge I see," Rosenthal whispered.

"I was looking for you," Coyle whispered to Suellen.

"You said we could walk together but didn't say where to meet or what time. I waited in the lobby for a while."

"This is a public trial," the judge scolded punctuated with a mallet bang. "If you have some secret evidence, you can tell us about, speak up."

"I was consulting with my client, Your Honor. I presume you don't have a problem with that.

Judge Avon's face blushed red, and he leered angrily over his spectacles.

The opening statements were brief. Both attorneys knew that everybody in Cripple Creek knew what had happened and had an opinion about it. Even in their short openings two different versions of the same event were described. The prosecution argued that the evidence was clear that Miss Suellen committed the crime; Coyle characterized the case as purely circumstantial with no proof of motive, no witnesses, and no physical evidence.

The first witness called was Cora Hewert. She looked prettier than when Coyle had interviewed her at the Old Homestead bordello. *She obviously had some extra money to spend on nicer clothes,* he thought.

R.A. Zang, assistant district attorney, opened with the usual questions, name, age, address, but left out profession.

Coyle started with questions that would be relevant to his case. "Do you know Suellen Miller?"

"I guess I know her as well as I know anyone else who lives in our boarding house. I was there when she signed the rental contract. No gentleman visitors, but if one did give the girl money, she had to give half of it to Misses DuPaulette. Like most, she signed the contract without reading it. They all thought they would marry some rich miner and not live at the Old Homestead House for any length of time."

"Did most of the residents, for example, Suellen Miller, know what they were in for?"

"They did if they read the rental agreement." Cora was starting to get uncomfortable.

Among scattered snickers around the room, Coyle proceeded.

"Do you like her?"

"No, I hate her. Always flouncing around like she is better than everybody else. Sleeping with Misses DuPaulette because she didn't want to sleep in the bed she worked in. All high and mighty."

"She's lying," Suellen whispered to Rosenthal. "I thought she was my friend."

Coyle was not showing the uneasiness on the outside that he was feeling. He had hoped Cora would testify to Sullen's good character. Coyle shifted gears.

"Did she take away any of your clients?" Coyle asked.

"She stole everybody's regular customers, she did. The rich ones she stole."

Coyle replied, "I've never been involved with your industry, but I assumed that would be quite common as your customers preferences changed."

The frown on Cora's face eased as she joined the snickers among the visitors. "Some of those yahoos don't know what they want."

"Was Miss Miller friendly with other residents of the boarding house?"

"Objection," J. A. Zang demonstrated that he was awake. "Calls for a subjective judgment on the part of the witness."

"Sustained." Judge Avon was happy to join the questioning.

"With Misses DuPaulette's demise did the residents of the

boarding house elect you to be the, shall we say, the traffic director?"

Cora Hewert laughed out loud. "We ain't no democracy. One of the pimps acted as a messenger. Some rich dude loaned the money to gussie-up the house the way Opal liked it. I don't know who, but I give a share of the profits to one of the boyfriends who gives it to the guy that loaned Opal the money. The messenger said the rich dude wanted me to get the job. So I became, let's say what it is, I am the madam."

"As the madam, would you have kicked Miss Miller out if her lawyer had not already suggested that she should find another place to reside until after this trial?"

"That is not true. She was one of the attractions. She made good money for her and for me. I don't make business decisions based on how much or whether I like a person or not."

Coyle leaned on the defense table. "Out of curiosity who is the messenger you pay your bribe to each week? What is his name?"

"Are you trying to get me shot? It was a loan that Opal borrowed and had to be paid back. I paid the messenger, and the rich guy hasn't complained that he didn't get his money."

After the instructions to the jury and the trial was over for the day, Coyle found a telephone at the Imperial Hotel front desk. The desk clerk said in a voice that was as phony as his smile, "Yes, of course you can use the telephone to call Colorado Springs, but please be brief, we get incoming calls from customers who need a room."

Coyle tried to turn his back to give the operator the long-distance number.

"This is your loving husband."

"I'm glad you called. The funniest thing just happened. The Lewises' cat found a warm spot where the afternoon sun shines through the window late in the day. It was a good place for a cat nap. Onie, you remember your daughter, don't you?"

"We haven't been apart for that long, sweetheart."

"Onie sneaked up on the sleeping cat and pulled its tail. The cat took off like a gun and Onie laughed. I wanted to laugh, too, but I had to scold her to satisfy Misses Lewis and Julie."

Coyle chuckled half-heartedly. He saw the desk clerk looking at him.

Sarah continued. "Yesterday Onie must have heard somebody say, 'There is more than one way to skin a cat,' because that is what Misses Lewis found Onie trying to do. I'm thinking our welcome is already wearing thin."

"Can you put Onie on?"

Sarah put out a sigh of regret and whispered, "She is being punished and I don't think the Lewises would appreciate the happy smiling face during her punishment."

Coyle knew he could not top the story of the tail pulling with his own story about the hostile witness he faced in court. He gave his love to all and hung up.

CHAPTER 21

The next morning, Coyle arrived at the hotel lobby ten minutes early according to the time and location that attorney and client had agreed to. Coyle was surprised to see Suellen was already sitting there prim and perky as usual.

On the street he was caught off guard when Suellen reached up and took his arm. She pulled it away as soon as she saw the uncomfortable look on his face.

"Sorry, I didn't want to make you feel uneasy," she said.

"No, it is just unusual. I have never had a client who wanted to walk arm in arm with me before. I didn't know what to do."

"I tell my men friends, just do what comes naturally," Suellen said quietly.

So, they chatted and walked up the Bennett Avenue hill. Mostly they talked about why Cora Hewert changed from Suellen's friend to hating her. Suellen said she didn't know Cora felt that way about her. Coyle explained that it was probably because of the job, and Cora was afraid Suellen might assume the role of madam.

Wagon drivers, carpenters, and bricklayers working on building repairs, could not afford a trip to the Old Homestead, but knew one of its vendors when they saw one. Other pedestrians on the street looked away in disgust at the curious couple. One person Coyle did not see, but who did notice Coyle, was Katie, the Coyles' previous neighbor and Sarah's friend. She seemed quite concerned and hurried down the street.

The observers were all settled in, the jury was seated, the prosecution and defense were at their appointed tables and the judge was announced and seated.

"The prosecution calls for Fred Woodward."

"Sometime later we will be talking with your brother, Harry. Would it be okay to call you Fred instead of Mister Woodward to avoid confusion?"

"No need to question both of us. He'll tell you the same thing. But okay."

"Now, Fred, you and your brother started the town of Victor. Is that right?

"Originally, we planned to use the land for a pasture for cattle. People were putting up shacks on our land. So, we got the land platted. Planned the streets and divided the lots. There was plenty of demand for houses and land to put them on. You might say we started Victor."

"And why was demand so great for land close to Money Mountain?" District Attorney P.A. Zang asked.

"The lots were being sold at a good rate. So, my brother decided to build a hotel for the overflow. In building the ground for a foundation he struck gold. That might be the reason the lots sold so quickly."

"Did you or your brother ever tell a person interested in buying a lot that every lot has a gold deposit under it?"

District Attorney Zang quickly followed with, "I know you can't answer for your brother, so I will ask you. Did you ever suggest that every lot in town had a gold deposit under it?"

"Certainly not. Not every lot." Fred Woodward said. "What does that have to do with the death of Opal DuPaulette?"

Judge Avon also wondered. "Yes, Mister Zang, what does that have to do with anything?"

"Mister Coyle put that witness's name on the list of witnesses, and I wanted to establish that the witness has been less than truthful in the past, Your Honor."

"Denied dealings in the past are not to be considered in this case. I think you knew that Mister Zang. The jury will disregard Fred Woodward's testimony up to this point."

"I have no further questions, Your Honor." The district attorney had a faint hint of a smile as he walked back to his place.

Fred Woodward stood to leave.

Coyle jumped to his feet. "Mister Woodward, if you don't mind, there are questions I would like to ask. Is it not true that you did not attend Opal DuPaulette's New Year's Eve party?"

Fred sat back down in the witness chair and straightened his coat. "Yes, that is true. I didn't go to that shindig."

"All mine owners and the richest businessmen were there. Did you not attend because you were not invited?"

"Of course, my brother and I were invited. We are Baptists and that is not the sort of place where a God lovin' man rings in the New Year. Besides, my wife was not feeling well, and I needed to be with her."

"When did you hear about Misses DuPaulette's death?"

"I can't say exactly when or who told me. I was at the Gold Coin Mine and all the miners were talking about it." Fred scratched his head and held his hands with the palms up in a gesture of that's all I can tell you.

In a few minutes Harry replaced Fred on the witness stand. District Attorney Zang established that Harry had attended the DuPaulette party, but only stayed long enough to eat supper. He quipped that he had never had caviar before and didn't like it. Harry did comment that Opal DuPaultte looked ravishing in her Paris ball gown, but he could not recall its color.

Coyle took a different tack. "Do you recall if any of the guests paid unusual attention to Misses DuPaulette? For example, danced with her more than one song?"

"Everyone was nice to her. Nice to her as they would be to any hostess that put on such a lavish and expensive party. Remember I was only there for dinner. Most of what my brother Fred told you is what I have to say."

"You served on the negotiation committee to end the strike. Do you see any connection to your work on that committee and the burning of the house you own that was occupied by me, who also was a part of the committee?"

"Objection, question asks the witness to make an opinion. And we are here to establish who killed Opal DuPaulette, not to discuss union business."

"Thank you, Mister Zang. Sustained."

Harry was flustered and flushed with anger. "You should have had to pay rent, and you could at least split the cost to rebuild."

Zang objected again and the judge banged his gavel. "Sustained."

Coyle persisted. "I believe Mister Rosenthal and your brother had an arrangement. But we have not asked for reimbursement for our personal property," Coyle answered. A gavel slammed down with a bang.

"Remember what this trial is about. One more aside and I'll charge you with contempt of court," the judge barked.

I asked for that one, Coyle thought. He walked back to the defense table to collect his thoughts, shuffling through some papers appearing to look for his next question.

"You and your brother, Fred Woodward, have bought several mines and claims. It appears that you are trying to block the way into Money Mountain—"

The gavel came up. Coyle raised his hand signaling for Judge Avon to wait until Coyle had a chance to ask his question.

"Did you ever intentionally or unintentionally tell Opal DuPaulette of your plans to take over the route into the Money Mountain Mining District. Or do you not recall?"

"I don't recall . . . I mean I didn't ever talk to Misses DuPaulette except to accept an invitation to her New Year's Eve party."

"Who did you tell of your plan to block the way into the Money Mountain District?"

"The people who sold their mines to us were satisfied. They got fair prices for what they had to sell," Harry said trying to dodge the question.

"No more questions for now, Your Honor." Coyle reserved the right to cross examine the witness.

"Court is adjourned until ten o'clock tomorrow morning."

CHAPTER 22

On the third day of the trial, Coyle and Suellen Miller were walking up Bennett Avenue hill to the courthouse. Suellen fretted that they might lose the trial and she might go to jail or even be hanged. The district attorney had brought in at least a dozen witnesses and none of them had seen anybody go into Opal DuPaulette's room except Suellen and Opal herself.

Suellen was doing most of the talking. Coyle was listening as he always did when a client was explaining why they should not lose their case. He might get some facts that he could use in his arguments. At the same time, his eyes were scanning the busy main business street of Cripple Creek.

The street was crowded with wagons carrying building materials, wagons with mining equipment, occasionally wagons with six mule-teams pulling loads of ore from the mines. Between the wagons there was the usual traffic of an occasional buggy or pedestrian.

Something caught Coyle's eye. He thought he saw his ex-neighbor Katie disappearing between two wagons and around the corner of Sully's fine foods store. Coyle stopped and turned around.

"What's wrong? Got a rock in your shoe?" Suellen asked.

Coyle smiled. "I thought I saw someone I know, a neighbor. I don't know why she didn't say hi or wave or something."

"Maybe she doesn't like the company you're keeping. I get a lot of that."

"Go ahead, you were saying you thought Opal liked you because you followed her instructions."

When Coyle called his name to testify, A.J. Tully looked like a kid caught by his mother raiding the cookie jar. His ears were pinned back, and he looked guiltily downward.

"What is your name, please?"

"A.J. Tully"

"Not initials, if you please."

"Everybody knows me as A.J. . . . okay, my name is Andrew James Tully. And what is your name?"

"Mister Coyle, attorney at law, and I ask the questions and you, Andrew James Tully, answer them, truly, fully, and to the best of your knowledge. Isn't that so Your Honor?"

Answered with a loud thump of the judge's mallet.

Coyle continued. "Did you know Misses DuPaulette?"

"Yes."

"Were you friends?"

"Opal has lots of friends . . . or had lots of friends."

"But you hoped that she considered you as a special friend. Is that correct, Mister Tully?"

"I asked her to marry me."

Rosenthal and Suellen Miller glared at each other with a *Did you know that?* look.

"Mister Tully, my family and I met you on the train from Denver transferring to Colorado Springs and then to Cripple Creek. Isn't that true?"

"We acknowledged each other, like strangers do on a train."

At the word "family," some unexplained instinct caused Coyle to turn around and glance at the audience. His quick survey of the faces stopped for an instant. There in the back row was Sarah sitting there in a new, green, plaid dress and her old blue overcoat, smiling imperceptibly at everyone but Coyle.

Coyle caught all those details in the blink of an eye and turned back to questioning Tully. "Yes, as you were saying, on the train. And what was your business in Denver?"

"I wanted to get some paperwork about deeds straightened out."

"And---?"

Tully paused for a few seconds, then decided Coyle knew the answer to the "and" question and he should go ahead and tell the truth. "Originally, I went to Denver to pick up a gown Opal ordered from Paris for the big New Year's Eve party. I shipped it to Cripple Creek in time for the party. Then a few days getting the paperwork straight as I told you."

"So, you were the anonymous donor for the gown?"

"And a couple other expenses for the party."

District Attorney Zang cross examined Tully, poking holes into the testimony, to steer the jury away from where he thought Coyle had tried to lead them.

Court was adjourned, and on his way out Rosenthal scolded, "What are you trying to do? Get my partner hanged for a crime he didn't commit? That wasn't the truth."

"It was all true," Coyle replied.

Coyle pushed his way through the crowd of men, mostly there to get a look at the glamorous and notorious Suellen Miller. He finally got through the crowd. "Sarah, what a surprise to see you here."

"Just wanted to watch my bright hubby at work."

At that moment, the crowd parted, and Suellen Miller walked through. Coyle called out, "See you at the same place and at the usual time."

Suellen answered, "Monday morning. Good day, Misses Coyle."

"She is nice and pretty too." *Even beautiful too,* Sarah thought.

"Where is Onie?" Coyle asked.

"She is at Katie's house. Their little girl is a little older but not as smart as Onie."

"My name is Leona but you can call me Onie," Coyle laughed.

"Katie said I could stay overnight at their house. Our Onie and our little family can have all day Saturday together. Katie called me on the telephone at the Springs and told me she said she saw you and Miss Miller walk to court together on two different mornings.

"Suellen is just a client. She is staying at the same hotel as me. Actually, her room is just across the hall from mine. So, it is natural that we walk up the hill together. That doesn't mean—"

"So, it is Suellen now. I don't like it." Sarah looked away.

CHAPTER 23

Coyle arrived at the appointed time at John and Katie's house to pick up Sarah and Leona. He couldn't help but see the scorch marks on the north side of the house. The burned beams, broken glass, and ashes from the house next door he had lived in had been cleared away and it looked like the site was being made ready for rebuilding.

For a short moment an image flashed through Coyle's mind of him running around with a garden hose trying to extinguish the blaze. *That would have been a good house to live in, if we had decided to stay in Cripple Creek,* he thought.

"For you Katie, thanks for being so kind to Sarah," Coyle said as he handed Katie a small bouquet of flowers.

"Thank you. Where did you get these? It is too early to have picked them. In the spring the whole hillside by Poverty Gulch is covered with flowers. These couldn't have come from there."

"There is a flower shop that opened about a block from the hotel," Coyle said.

She looked at the flowers with admiration. "I didn't know there was a flower shop in town. Who can afford to buy flowers in Cripple—" She stopped when she realized she might have offended Coyle. Katie gestured for Coyle to come in.

"Where is John?" Coyle asked. Just then Sarah and Leona walked in accompanied by Mable, the little girl that Onie was so happy to see. There were not many kids Onie's age in Colorado Springs, so the child was delighted to see her friend.

"John is out playing baseball of all things. You would think he would grow up." Katie whirled around and started for the kitchen. As she passed Sarah she winked. "I'll find something to put these in."

"Meg can come with us, can't she?" Onie asked anxiously.

"If she wants to," Coyle said. "If her mother says it is okay."

The happy little group left on a Saturday outing.

"Let's catch the train and go up to Victor. I've heard there are a couple of good restaurants there and the scenery is beautiful."

Victor was a smaller town than Cripple Creek, but big enough to have schools including a high school, and a park with a baseball field with a stadium of sorts.

The train ride was indeed beautiful. Sarah spent most of her time looking out the window. The two girls, Onie, and Meg were paying more attention to one of Meg's dolls.

After having trout for lunch, they walked over to the baseball stadium because they heard cheers coming from there. "Let's go see John play baseball," Sarah exclaimed.

Coyle was surprised because Sarah was not interested in sports beyond an occasional game of Rook at the card table after dinner. Coyle didn't consider that a sport. Nevertheless, Coyle was glad to see Sarah take an interest in something he also enjoyed.

"Good, the Hoosiers are playing against the Black Sox. I see John is the pitcher. Do you want to wave and say hello to your father, Meg?"

"Daddy doesn't want to be bothered when he is playing baseball."

As they took their seats Sarah tugged on Coyle's arm and asked, "That team is wearing black stockings, that's why they are called the Black Sox. I get that, but why are several of them carrying sticks?"

"Those are called bats. When it is their turn, each one uses their bat to try and hit the ball that John, the pitcher, throws to them. If they hit the ball, they can run to first base over there. If the ball goes far away, they might run to second base or even to third base." Coyle used his hands to indicate the places was describing.

"After the runner goes to all three bases, he tries to run home."

"He doesn't get to play anymore? He has to go home?" Sarah asked.

"No. They stay in the game. Going home means they score a run. Whoever scores the most runs wins."

Sarah looked confused.

"Look at that. The batter hit the ball over the fence. The runners on base get to go home and the batter gets to run around all the bases because he hit a home run."

Sarah stated, "That's a silly game. You say they play baseball all the time in the big cities in the East?"

"It is very popular in the East. In New York and Boston, they have played baseball since before I was born," Coyle said.

"Where are the girls?" Sarah said as she suddenly discovered the two girls were missing. "They were right here. Leona wouldn't go off and leave the sock doll that we made together from a sock of yours. One that didn't have a hole in it. She wouldn't leave it behind and go somewhere." Sarah screamed so loud that spectators in the next section of the grand stadium could hear her. "ONIE!"

Coyle grimaced at the spectacle and was starting to wish he had never heard about the Victor baseball stadium. He looked between the rows of seats and saw the ground below. Remembering how he liked to play in the dirt at that age, he thought that would be a good place to look for the girls. It crossed his mind that he got in trouble for getting his clothes dirty in those days. He hoped Onie wouldn't get her new dress coat as dirty as he had his Sunday school clothes because Onie's mother didn't have a housekeeper like Coyle's mother had.

"Sarah, please stay here with Sock Eye. Meg is old enough to remember where we were sitting. They will probably be back before I am. I will go look under the bleachers to see if they went down there to play in the dirt."

Years ago, Coyle would have enjoyed looking up at all the fannies hanging over the bleacher seats. That day all he could think of was where Onie and her friend Meg could have slipped away to . . . and were they safe. After looking and walking halfway around the stadium, he decided to check with Sarah to see if she had seen the girls.

As soon as Coyle came out from under the bleachers, there stood Onie and Meg a half a dozen yards away. Coyle ran to them and dropped to his knees. He gave them a group hug. He stood up and looked them over top to bottom. No dirt, clean as before.

"Where have you scallywags been? We have been looking for you."

Onie answered first. "I had to go potty."

Meg explained, "There was not enough money to build the modern indoor ones, but I knew where the old ones were, so I took her there."

Coyle covered up his relief with strong words. "Leona, you know you are supposed to tell Mommy or me where you are going. This time tell Mommy that I found you."

Meg said, "Her Mother already knows. We went to her when we got done at the potty. She told us to look for you."

Onie held up her sock doll, Sock Eye, as proof.

CHAPTER 24

Coyle carefully explained the legal import of his baseball stadium story to his wife as they walked to a park playground where their daughter and her friend could frolic.

"In July of '95, Joe Fox read an article announcing the secretary of agriculture had allowed beef to come across the Mexican border to Texas without paying import taxes in order to bring down the price of beef.

"Fox and his money-making schemes were well known. In Cripple Creek the population tolerated him because the wild scams were funny, and hardly anyone fell for them anyway. One day Fox left for Texas. Joe Fox came back with a black sombrero, tight black pants, a black jacket with silver buttons on it, and a contract with a matador. The contract included all the players in the drama of man against the bull and best of all, four fighting bulls."

He paused as the girls dashed to the swing set, asking to be pushed higher. Sarah gave Coyle a subtle *No* look, and he continued.

"The president of the county Humane Association took a petition to the sheriff, who sent it to the governor, who sent the petition back to the Humane Association without comment. The bullfight was on."

"On the day of the big event there was a parade. Senor Jose Fox, who had added a black cape with a red lining to his wardrobe, rode in a carriage. He was followed by a carriage carrying the matador. Walking behind came the banderilleros, picadors, and four heavy carts, each with a bull inside."

Coyle paused the story again, telling Sarah they had better get back to the train station in case the train to Cripple Creek left early. It was too far to walk. As they got ready to leave, a shot rang out and Coyle fell, but regained his feet gingerly.

"I'm alright. Is everyone okay?" Sarah nodded and then Coyle dashed to where he thought the shot came from. Coyle felt off balance, started to limp, and then stopped. He looked at his boots and got the surprise of the day. Someone had shot the heel off. Sarah ran to her husband, thinking he was wounded.

"I'm lucky whoever did this is not a very good shot."

"Or maybe he's a damn good one," Sarah said. "Maybe it's a warning of some sort. Consider me warned. Let's get out of here."

Back on the train, wife, two children, and one doll, were all accounted for. Coyle leaned back and started to relax, wondering who might have shot at him, and why. The girls were as giggly and busy as ever. Coyle had to admit being a lawyer was easier the herding children. Even two were a handful. Slowly the spruce trees began to dance past the window.

Sarah leaned against Coyle. "All of these shootings and the fires . . . it's become too much, Andrew. Someone is going to get seriously hurt."

"If someone wanted me dead I would be in the ground by now. I think it's just intimidation, and I can't let that keep me from doing my job. Now relax, my dear, and let me finish my story."

"Okay, what happened next? The parade and Senor Jose and bulls in carts. You were telling me all about it."

"Oh, yes. This is just what I was told had happened. In the afternoon people came from all over. There was a special train from Denver loaded with people wanting to see the first bullfight ever in the United States. All the streets and roads that crossed the route to Victor were blocked."

"Soapy Smith came from Denver to sell phony tickets to the bullfight. The Victor baseball stadium we visited was full. Over five hundred tickets were sold. Of course, the stadium doesn't hold that many people, but that didn't bother Soapy."

"There was a special high seat next to where the bulls were to come out. That's where Jose Fox chose to announce the activities."

Onie's friend Mable said, "A hundred. That's one with two zeros behind it."

Coyle didn't know the kids were listening, but when he found out he had an audience he was encouraged to continue.

"The bull was let into the ring where the matador stood waving his red cape. The bull was very mad because the rancher whom Fox arranged to feed the bulls would not provide the hay on credit. After a few charges at the cape but not the matador, the bull was tired. The matador brought out a big and very sharp sword. He hid the sword behind the cape and waved it to attract the bull one last time. The bull charged and at the last second the matador thrust the sword into the bull and killed it. The crowd cheered. Some booed because they didn't know about bullfighting, but the same could be said of the spectators who cheered."

"An assistant matador did the same to a second bull, only with fewer ballet moves and a plainer costume. The spectators were less enthusiastic."

"That was just awful. It was just so cruel," Sarah said.

"Joe Fox said it was not nearly as cruel as what the rancher did when he wouldn't feed the bulls on credit when they came all the way from Texas." Coyle paused. "Only fifty spectators paid on the second day. Fox called off the third day. Creditors came to see him on the fourth day. Joe Fox was out of town and had no forwarding address when the sun came up on the fifth day."

"Good riddance," Sarah added.

Coyle concluded with, "The person who told me about the bullfighting ring in the baseball stadium said that Fox is managing a fancy restaurant in Florida. And he still brags about being the person who staged the one and only bullfighting exhibition in the United States."

"Who told you that? Your friend from across the hall in the hotel?"

Luckily, the train pulled into the Cripple Creek station before Coyle could answer.

"Katie has asked me to stay over at her and John's house until the trial is over, but there isn't room for you. There isn't really enough room for Leona and me," Sarah said. Then she added, "Truthfully the Lewis's are not very pleased about Onie and the cat. Although they are very cordial about the incident. The cat stays under the bed all day and most of the night."

They passed from the spruce and pine trees and then from aspen starting to bud, which would turn into leaves in the warmth of summer. The train passed a handful of holes in the ground and other abandoned mines and finally into the terminal.

"We might go back to the Lewis's tomorrow, I don't know." Sarah walked away. After a few steps she turned and said, "Why don't you get a shave. You look terrible."

Coyle mumbled, "At least you got to see the stadium where the only bullfight ever in the United States was held." He was not sure anyone had heard him.

Coyle set out to find a shoe repair shop where he could get a heel put on his boot and since he liked his red beard, he resolved not to shave until the beard got in the way of his vest.

CHAPTER 25

Monday morning Coyle telephoned Barton Rosenthal, waking him.

"Good morning, Bart."

"What do ya want?"

"Remember I let you sit with me at the defense table during the trial, because you hired me, and you might be qualified, and the judge agreed?"

"So, you don't need me anymore?"

"That's not why I'm calling. I have a favor to ask of you. Sarah is picky about whom I am seen with on the street. No reason, it is just her thing. I was wondering if you could meet Suellen at her hotel and walk with her up to the courtroom."

"The hotel? Did you mean *our* hotel? You randy rascal." Rosenthal chuckled in a way Coyle hated. "I'm sorry, Andy ol' boy. Julia is getting serious, so I should not walk anywhere with your client. You can understand, can't you? You can telephone my partner Tully. He has no woman problems. And he does have a telephone now."

With the operator's help Coyle got Tully's number. "Hello A.J., your partner Rosenthal suggested that you might be able to help me."

"Yes, I might," Tully's voice was icy.

"I need somebody to meet Suellen Miller to escort her to the courtroom."

Tully answered right away. "You've got me on your witness list. I don't think I should walk into court with your client. It might indicate a conflict of interest."

Suellen noticed that Coyle was unusually quiet as they walked up Bennett Avenue. He didn't have that old rah-rah, let's-go-win-this-case spirit.

"You're awfully quiet this morning. Did you get enough sleep?"

Coyle didn't answer right away. When he did speak up, he said, "I don't lose sleep over any cases I have in court." It was the best he could do.

Suellen thought quietly as they walked. Finally, she said, "Are you worried because you think we are losing the case?"

"No, it's nothing." Coyle smiled weakly.

"Woman problems. Men always say it is nothing when they have woman problems."

"My wife . . . she's uncomfortable with what people might think when they see me walking with you."

"What do you think." Suellen had a cute, perhaps even flirtatious, way of tilting her head to one side. Coyle tried not to notice.

"What I think doesn't matter, but if it did, I would be worried about what people would think if I did not walk with my client. It might be seen as an admission of guilt."

"I get a lot of that, what people might think." What she said next sounded like something she had been thinking about, but she had not had anybody to admit it to in a confidential conversation. "My father only let me go through second grade. My oldest brother got to go through eighth grade, and two other brothers went to sixth grade. A girl has to make a living. I couldn't get a good job like a salesclerk or a bank teller. So, I went where I could make the most money. And it didn't matter that I can't hardly read."

Suellen clearly had more to say, but they had arrived at the building being used as a courthouse until a real courthouse could be built. Coyle straightened his tie. Suellen stood in front of the door waiting for Coyle to open it for her.

———◆———

Suellen and Rosenthal sat quietly at the defense table as Coyle went through the papers he had brought in a cloth bag that served as a briefcase. He shuffled and reshuffled the pages of witness's names, key questions from the prosecution, and witness's answers, and questions he intended to ask.

The reshuffling routine was interrupted by the court clerk who announced, "Witness number thirty-eight, Mike Calterrock, president of Western Miners Union, are you here? Witness Calterrock, are you here?" No response.

The clerk came over to the defendant's table and spoke quietly to Coyle. "Your witness Mister Calterrock is in Leadville on Union business. I gave him one more chance to show up. Guess you have to scratch him off your witness list. I'll tell Mister Zang."

"I wanted him as a character witness. Win one for the prosecutor, Mister Zang."

"Too bad, there are many union men here today. You would get an appreciative audience." The clerk excused himself and went over to the prosecution desk.

Coyle thought, *It's true, when there is a jury, it is better to have the audience on your side.*

Zang looked over from the prosecutor's table with a coy smile. He had already heard the news.

———◆———

When called, Tully took the stand. He answered all the preliminary questions. Judge Avon looked like he was in a good mood. Coyle had a feeling this would be a good testimony.

"Did you know Opal DuPaulette?"

"I know lots of people, and she was one of them."

"Did you attend her holiday party?"

"No." Tully hesitated. "I was in Denver."

"Is it true you financed the party?"

"I gave her ten thousand dollars, but I did not pay the five hundred dollars that the people who went to the party did."

"So, you paid ten thousand but didn't go to the party?" Coyle heard some murmurs in the audience.

"You know, I came on the same train from Denver that you and your family did."

"The night of the explosion at the terminal annex, you were a big help to the people on the train and people at the station. That is where we met, is it not?"

"Yes."

"Isn't ten thousand a lot to pay for not going to a party?"

"It paid for Opal's gown and part of the champagne. I didn't mind. She looked beautiful at her funeral."

"But you didn't go to the party?"

"No, I did not."

In later testimony, two employees, Honey B and Cozy Rosey, of the Old Homestead House, corroborated Suellen's friendship with Opal DuPaulette. There were to have been three testifying, but the third one had been beaten up by a customer and was in the hospital. The customer was out of jail on bond. After their testimony, the bailiff stood to call the next witness. Coyle interrupted with a request to speak to the judge.

District Attorney Zang stood shoulder to shoulder with Coyle as they faced the judge and out of hearing distance of the jury and the spectators.

"What is it, Mister Coyle?" Judge Avon said with a no-nonsense tone.

"It is late, and I do not think we have enough time to properly question the next witness."

"I don't have a problem with it," said Zang, clearly not wanting to agree with anything Coyle requested.

"We had a two-hour recess for lunch. You can surely put in some overtime now." Judge Avon peered down at Coyle.

"To the point, the next witness has not been told that his testimony has been requested. I only call on him because two witnesses did not appear today."

Zang jumped in with, "The defense attorney wants more time to coach the witness."

"May I remind you, Mister Coyle, that you are scheduled to be on trial yourself in a couple of weeks, and we need to wrap up this trial expeditiously."

"I did nothing wrong, and I am prepared to stand trial. I will defend myself."

"A lawyer who defends himself has a fool for a client. Request denied." The gavel spoke with a loud bang!

CHAPTER 26

It had been a long day for Andrew Coyle and now he had to interview the one person he didn't want to question. Coyle walked back to the defense table. He looked up at the bailiff and nodded.

The audience seemed to be exceptionally quiet as the bailiff announced, "The defense calls Barton Rosenthal."

Rosenthal sat up from his slouch and went into the look of a soldier at attention. His head jerked around toward Coyle as though he had been ordered to do a dress-right-dress.

"You didn't tell me you were going to call me as a witness," Rosenthal hissed.

"I didn't know two other witnesses wouldn't show up."

Rosenthal was sworn in, and Coyle established the witness's name, occupation, and place of residence.

"Did you attend Opal DuPaulette's New Year's Eve party?"

"Yes."

"Did you leave early?"

"Yes."

"Would you say you left at about ten o'clock? Isn't that true?"

"Maybe a few minutes after that. I was saying goodbye to everyone, but I wanted to catch the ten-twenty train to the Springs. They don't run very often at night, 'specially New Years."

"Did you see anyone on the train who could identify you?"

Rosenthal paused for a minute. "The conductor. He was sorry he had missed the entire New Year's Eve celebration because he had to work."

"Isn't it true that your friend Suellen Miller didn't express any remorse or surprise over Misses DuPaulette's death? And didn't she tell you she had been asleep during the whole thing?

"Not my *friend*, just an acquaintance. No, she didn't . . . and she said she was glad she didn't sneak some sleeping powder like she had sometimes done."

"Mister Rosenthal, can you tell me why she was glad she did not sneak sleeping powder from Misses DuPaulette's container?"

"The doctor who signed the death certificate said that the sleeping powder container was mixed with coca ethylene, or something like that. It is found in rat poison. It is bad stuff. The jeweled sleeping powder container had enough rat poison in it to kill a horse, let alone a person. That's why she said that," Rosenthal answered.

Coyle had to pause while the judge's mallet tried to quiet the audience.

"I happened to be at the National Hotel for their grand opening. It was approximately three weeks after Misses DuPaulette's passing. You rode into the hotel bar on your horse. And riding behind you was Suellen Miller. Would you agree that that is an unusual way to mourn the death of a friend and employer?"

BANG! The mallet came down with a resounding thump. "You are asking for an opinion. In addition, that question is totally inappropriate."

"No more questions, Your Honor." Coyle knew he shouldn't have asked that question, but it didn't hurt that the jury had heard it.

"Your witness, mister district attorney."

"No more questions," said Zang with that annoying little smile that always bothered Coyle.

"You may step down."

Rosenthal wasted no time in getting out of the witness chair and off the stand. He practically ran up the aisle passing his usual place at the defense table. The door slammed after him. Scattered quiet laughter spread through the room. Most of the audience didn't know if they were allowed to laugh or not.

As the crowd slowly dispersed, Coyle spotted someone that made him drop what he was doing and take another look. Sure enough, there was Sarah Coyle standing behind the back row of seats with the trace of a smile. Her expression said she wasn't sure if she was welcome there.

Coyle rushed around a small group standing in the aisle discussing the case. Upon reaching her, Coyle gave Sarah a big hug and peck on the cheek.

"I didn't expect to see you here, but I'm glad you came," he said.

"Of course, I'm here. I don't want people shooting at my husband and knocking the heel off his boot when I'm not there to protect him."

"How were you going to protect me?" Coyle quipped.

"Julie Lewis offered me the use of a lady's small pistol to keep in my handbag in case I needed it. Naturally, I told her I would be just as likely to shoot myself as I would be to shoot some assassin."

Coyle saw Suellen with Cora Hewert passing by. He caught her eye and quietly said, "I'll see you here tomorrow. Don't forget, you're out on bond and not allowed to leave town."

"Why don't you walk her back to the hotel you two share," Sarah said. "I'm okay. I can take care of myself. You don't need to worry about me."

———◆———

That night Coyle tossed and turned in his bed wrapped in a tangle of blankets and sheets. He decided to review the testimony from the day. He could remember it almost line for line. He had gotten no help from the two or three women talking and laughing across the hall. Ironically, something they said made him relax and go to sleep. Sleep with a plan for the next day in mind.

CHAPTER 27

Coyle caught up with Rosenthal in his office where he confronted him with, "Come on, Bart, you know I had to put a witness on the stand or say we have no further evidence and let the DA close the case."

"Right after you threw me under the stagecoach, I went down to the telephone to call Julie to explain what she had already heard from friends who were at the trial." Rosenthal let out a long, loud sigh. "She won't talk to me. It was bad enough she heard I rode a horse into the National Hotel bar. Why did you have to mention that Suellen was riding behind me on the horse?"

"Half of Cripple Creek Mining District was there in the bar. The same people were in court yesterday. If I hadn't pointed out that the two of you were on the horse, I might have gotten charged with withholding evidence. Besides, if I didn't mention that fact, Zang would have."

Rosenthal mumbled some expletives.

———◆———

Coyle and Rosenthal were mostly silent as they walked up the hill to the building that had previously housed a clothing and hardware store and had been converted to the Teller County courthouse.

Along the way, Rosenthal asked, "What's that you're carrying?"

"A little prop that might make a point in somebody's testimony. We'll see."

"Looks like rain or snow or both. Typical Cripple Creek spring weather," Rosenthal said.

Silence prevailed for the rest of the walk. Coyle was not surprised to see Suellen already sitting at the defendant's table when they arrived. She looked up from reading *The Colorado Springs Gazette* with a welcoming smile.

"Look here, they've got a picture of us, me and you on the front page."

"Don't we look nice?" Coyle rolled his eyes.

Rosenthal chimed in with, "Now look at who is in the doghouse."

The bailiff made all the required announcements. Judge Samuel Avon entered, all stood, and court was in session.

The first witness called was the train conductor from the night train between Colorado Springs and Cripple Creek.

"Mister Butler, were you the conductor on the train from Cripple Creek to Colorado Springs on December 31, New Year's. Eve?"

"Yes."

Coyle pointed at Rosenthal. "Do you recognize that man, Mister Rosenthal?"

"Yes, he looks familiar. I've seen him before."

"Did Mister Barton Rosenthal travel on your train the night of December 31?"

Butler was still in uniform from his conductor's job. He turned his conductor hat around in his hands before he answered. Butler looked at Rosenthal.

"There were many more riders on the train that night. I cannot say . . . yes, now I remember. Mister Rosenthal is a regular rider. He goes to the Springs many times a week. That night I told him I didn't get to have fun 'cause I was working on New Year's Eve. And

Mister Rosenthal, he said to me, working and making money is more important than having a good time."

"What time was he on your train?"

Butler pulled out a large, round, railroad watch and said, "We just passed the *grande curve*, so I guess it would be around ten past ten if we were on time."

"So, it was about ten-ten when you talked to Mister Rosenthal on the train?"

"Yes, if we were on time. But I guess it was ten twenty-eight when I talked to Mister Rosenthal."

"No further questions, Your Honor."

Zang said, "No questions, Your Honor. Let the poor man get some sleep."

The bailiff said, "The next witness is Mister Ned Boatwright. Calling Mister Boatwright, witness."

"Boatwright, may I call you by your commonly used nickname Boats?" Coyle asked.

"Aye."

"Is it Boats because your family name is Boatwright?"

"It is because I was a boatswain's mate in His Majesty's Navy."

Coyle scratched his head. "Isn't this an odd place for a sailor?"

"My enlistment was up when our ship landed in Frisco. The captain assumed I would stay on the ship 'til we got to England. But not me. I got off the ship and picked up an oar. Slung it over my shoulder and started walking inland until somebody asked me, 'What's that you're carrying on your shoulder?' I said this is the place. And here I am in Cripple Creek."

The room broke out in laughter—even the judge.

"Okay everyone, settle down," the judge said, still grinning.

Coyle continued his questioning. "May I ask what your dry land occupation is?"

"Human relations. A man who is lonely can come to me and I use my knowledge and experience to see that the man and a suitable woman get together. I even take the man to the woman's current address."

"Am I correct in assuming that address is the Old Homestead boarding house?"

"Quite often that is correct. I work at the railroad warehouse issuing parts and building supplies. Old Homestead is right across the street. It is a natural place to send a lonely man."

"Is it true you collect tips for this information?"

"Quite often I make arrangements for the customer, er client, so they don't have to haggle."

"I have witnesses who will more precisely will say what you do if you don't wish to admit it."

Boats squirmed.

"Okay, I'm an agent for a few of the girls at Old Homestead. But I also served as a go-between messenger for Misses DuPaulette. You see, Winston Sullivan loaned Misses DuPaulette money to fix up the house. I took DuPaulette's weekly repayment to Mister Sullivan because he didn't want women to carry that much money.

"Are you saying he trusted you?"

"Why do you think he got so many haircuts? Misses DuPaulette would go out every week or two and report how much business they took in and what his share should be."

"I assume you had given him the right amount."

"Every penny."

The district attorney jumped up. "I object. We are not trying Winston Sullivan or Mister Ned Boatwright. Mister Coyle has not shown how Sullivan or Boats have any connection to Opal DuPaulette's murder."

"If it pleases the Court, there have been two murders," Coyle said. "Both victims were in a business relationship that involved a great deal of money. The defense is trying to establish a motive and an opportunity for someone other than the accused, Miss Miller, who happened to be sleeping at the time of the murder."

"Sustained. If you have a point here, please make it or we must move on."

Coyle nodded in deference and continued.

"Boats, as an employee of the Old Homestead, did you go to the New Year's Party?"

"No, wasn't invited."

Judge Avon was already reaching for his gavel.

"Did Mister Sullivan ever tell you to make Miss Cora Hewert the new madam at Homestead after Misses DuPaulette's death?"

"Not directly."

"Did he say that indirectly?"

"No." Boatwright again started squirming. "But he knew Cora and I are married."

"No more questions," Coyle said.

"No more questions, but the prosecution reserves the right to recall Mister Boatwright," said Zang.

CHAPTER 28

After lunch, there was a big crowd waiting outside the courthouse door. Inside, all the seats were filled, and people stood against the wall on either side of the room. Two extra deputies were called in to keep the aisles open.

Suellen Miller was escorted into the courtroom by two deputies. She had used her lunch break to comb her blonde hair up into an even tighter knot on top of her head, and she had washed most of the makeup from her face. Suellen's clothing had been neat, clean, and thoroughly plain throughout the trial, but now she had buttoned the top button of her dress. It looked like it was choking her. To top off the whole illusion, she wore a white cardigan thrown casually over her shoulders and carried an umbrella in deference to the gray threatening sky.

Coyle looked up, and then looked away quickly. He didn't want to get caught staring at his pretty client knowing his wife might be watching. *I can understand how some men might find her attractive,* he said to himself. *Admit it. You and every man in this room might find her attractive. And now I'm ashamed to be talking to myself.*

Rosenthal was not so reserved. He leaned over and whispered to

Coyle. "Hot damn, are all of your clients that pretty?"

Without looking up, Coyle responded, "Not all, Bart. You hired me once, which would make you my client."

Suellen took her seat at the defense table.

"Hi, there. Are you my two handsome defenders? Do your job and keep me out of jail." Suellen flashed that cute little smile and crinkled her nose.

"I hope you are just joking. Did someone escort you from the hotel to the courthouse?"

"My previous escort was afraid to be seen with me. I came by myself."

"Most people on trial for murder are kept in jail. You are lucky to be out on bail. You can thank Mister Rosenthal for that. I strongly suggest you are always with somebody when you go out of the hotel."

Before Suellen could answer, the bailiff announced Judge Samuel Avon. The judge looked startled when he saw the standing-room-only crowd. He sat and immediately banged his gavel.

"Order in the court. Everyone whose name is on the witness list go to the witness room across the hall." Four people reluctantly headed toward a side door.

One raised his hand and asked, "The people who already witnessed or the ones who are going to witness? Who are you talking about?"

"Your name is on the list. Go to the witness room." Judge Avon leered at the crowd. "Everyone who does not have a seat, please leave the building. Your friends will tell you if you missed anything." Addressing the sheriff's deputies he added, "Make sure they all get out the door."

Coyle and Rosenthal looked at each other with almost as much disbelief as the exiting spectators. Suellen Miller sat quietly, her expression shifting nervously from nonchalance to impatience, as if she had more important things to do.

District Attorney Zang had a half sneer, half confident smile.

The bailiff called for the next witness, Miss Suellen Miller.

Coyle whispered to Suellen, "Remember, you are the defendant. That means you don't have to say anything that self-incriminates."

"I don't have nothin' to hide." Suellen stood.

After the swearing in, Suellen sat in the witness chair and crossed her legs folding her long skirt under her lap. Someone let out a loud whistle, which brought numerous chuckles from among the crowd.

The gavel spoke for Judge Avon. "That man with a blue checkered shirt-jacket." Avon said as he pointed at the whistler. "Escort him to the door and detain him. Let one person in to take the rowdy one's seat. We will have order in this court."

Security guards took charge of the man who had interrupted.

Suellen was reminded that she had sworn to tell the truth the whole truth and nothing but the truth. Coyle asked all the obligatory questions, spelling of name, address of residence, time of living there. Coyle skipped the question about occupation.

"Is it true that you are the most recent hire at the Old Homestead?"

"That's true unless somebody was hired after you told me to move out to a more respectable place of residence. You told me that meant a place to live until after the trial."

Zang looked at Rosenthal as a sign that he had scored some points without getting out of his chair. His smile was even less friendly than his taciturn demeanor.

"You must have been good friends with Misses DuPaulette if she let you sleep in her bedroom and bed. Is that true?"

Suellen answered without pause. "She was the boss, and I was the employee. She understood my feelings about sleeping where I worked. We were never close friends."

"Did you know when she left the party and came to the bedroom?"

"She was singing *There will be a hot time in Cripple Creek duh da duh da* . . . If somebody knows when the group was singing that, it will tell you what time she came to bed."

"Did she share what was in the little jeweled box in the dresser drawer?"

"That was only morphine. You can buy morphine down at the drug store. Opal shared some chocolate cake that she had juiced up. I had a couple pieces of cake at different times. The cake was good. I snuck some of that on a couple occasions when I had bad tricks. You have to take the bad with good. Opal taught me that."

"Is the reason you were employed at Old Homestead House that you saw more good than bad in it?"

Suellen tensed for just a moment. "There is lots of money out there if you are willing to do what you need to do to get it."

Coyle thought, *Like being a lawyer.*

"Let's go back a few years. Did you and your family move often?"

"Objection. That question has no relevance to Mises DuPaulette's death," Zang said.

"If you are trying to make a point Mister Coyle you better make it," Judge Avon scolded.

Coyle gave Zang a look that said, *You dared me.*

Coyle pulled a package he had brought to court that morning out from under the defense table. He tore off the brown wrapping paper showing a three-by-three poster with handwritten sentences painted on it.

"Now, Miss Miller, have you ever seen this poster before?"

"No, where would I see something like that?"

Coyle turned around and showed the poster to the jury. He took particular interest in showing it to Zang. "I didn't plan in advance to spring this on you. Last night I was thinking of ways to make the situation clear. I came up with this idea and persuaded the night registrar to help me. If you have some props to help make your case I would be happy to consider how fair they might be." Then he turned back to face Suellen before Zang could answer.

"Miss Miller, please read the top line."

Suellen smiled sheepishly. "See the dog . . . ummm . . . the cat."

"Good, now the second line."

"The big dog and the min . . . cat."

"Good, you can guess at the words you don't know. Now read the third line, please."

"The doctor wrote a *pre . . . scrib . . .* note for the *pat . . . person.*" Suellen looked at Coyle and her eyes said, *please no more.* She blushed. *I have never been so humiliated.*

"Good, now the last one sentence." Coyle uncovered sentence four. "Please read the bottom line."

"Dagger, a picture of skull and crossbones, then it says, Murfin . . . doctor's . . . *dir . . . ugggh . . . faythol . . .* I am sorry. I don't know what it says, Mister Coyle."

"In case anybody wonders, the sentences were, 'See the dog chase the cat.' The second line, 'The big dog and the mini cat.' The third line, 'The doctor wrote a prescription for the patient.' And the bottom line, 'Danger,' then the picture, and the text says, 'Morphine, follow doctor's directions. Lethal if misused.'"

"Is it true that you family moved quite often when you were a child?"

"Yes."

"Is it true that you moved often from school to school?"

"No, sir," Suellen answered succinctly.

Slightly thrown off by not getting the answer he expected, Coyle asked again. "Then how many schools did you attend?"

"One, I went to one school for both of my years in school. One school, one teacher, both years. I was almost at the top of my class. There was one boy who had been there four years. He did better than me."

"Did your father want you to go to school?"

"No. Pap said people with too much education were not any smarter than him, but they didn't know it."

"And only one brother went as far as eighth grade?"

"The other two brothers went to sixth grade. Pap said the boys were too young to work for wages, but after sixth grade they were big enough to do lots of jobs on the farm. But girls could get by if they could make a meal for their family out of possum stew and turnip greens."

Coyle changed his location in order to be where he would be able to look at Suellen and without turning his head much, he could also observe Zang.

"Would it be correct for me to say that if you held a bottle of medicine, you would not know if it was poison or not by reading the label?"

"Sometimes I would know. Most of the time doctors use such big words," replied Suellen.

Zang erupted.

"Objection! She did not answer the question. Did she or did she not know if the little jeweled container contained poison?"

Judge Avon answered immediately. "You are out of order, Mister Zang. Mister Coyle was making a point about the defendant's ability to read. You may proceed Mister Coyle, and you, Mister Zang, are overruled. Court stenographer, please strike the DA's statement from the record."

Coyle was glad he did not have to answer Zang's objection. He moved forward before the judge changed his mind.

"Miss Miller, did you know when Misses DuPaulette came into the bedroom the night she died?"

"I could hear the noise from the banquet room. The door was open for a few seconds. I hardly saw anything because the light hurt my eyes. Can I say something?"

"Yes, of course, you swore to tell the whole truth."

"When the door was open, I kept my eyes shut and I played like I was asleep because I didn't want to get involved. But I went back to sleep because my eyes were closed."

"Are you known as a heavy sleeper so a person would believe you were asleep?"

"I don't know what people say about me, but I was asleep shortly after she closed the door. Yes, when I closed my eyes, I really did go to sleep. I wasn't pretending."

"So, just to be perfectly clear," Coyle concluded, "you went straight to bed and to sleep and only woke up long enough to know Misses DuPaulette came into the room?"

"Yes, that is what happened."

"No more questions, Your Honor."

Zang bored right in.

"Did you read the lease agreement contract when you rented a room in the Old Homestead and, in fact, became an employee at the same time?"

"There was no contract. Misses DuPaulette told me I would pay her half of everything I earned, and she would set the rates depending on how popular I was. For that I got a room and two meals a day. That is not too bad if you are dieting and watching your figure."

A few spectators giggled.

"Could you guess about what time it was when Misses DuPaulette came into her bedroom? Was it before or after everyone sang *Should Old* or after when everyone was kissing?"

"I was instructed to tell the truth, the whole truth, and nothing but the truth. I think that would mean not guessing. I was asleep, so I couldn't guess."

Zang's trap had failed. "No more question, Your Honor."

After Suellen was excused and returned to her seat at the defendant's table, Coyle took a long look at her. Suellen nodded in a whisper of a gesture.

Coyle snapped into action. If anybody had studied his physical communication, they would have said that in that second, he made a decision. "We have no more witnesses, Your Honor."

Zang repeated the same. He kept open the caveat that he had the right to recall witnesses if discrepancies or conflicts were discovered.

A gray overcast gave way to black rain clouds. A slow but constant drizzle set in and was punctuated by occasional snowflakes, but very few onlookers left the crowd around the courthouse entrance.

"We will take a short recess. Upon our return we will hear the counselors' closing arguments."

CHAPTER 29

There were a few empty seats for the onlookers now. A deputy sheriff let a small group from outside come in. It seemed to give him a great deal of pleasure to be ordering people around. The people coming in were just happy to have a dry seat inside. Those without seats were told to leave.

"All rise. Court of Teller County now in session, Judge Samuel Avon presiding." There was the sound of water dripping on the floor in a few places in the room.

Judge Avon looked over the top of the glasses perched on the tip of his nose. "The prosecution will present their closing argument first and have opportunity go last and point out any discrepancies in the testimonies or the closing. I assume those will be minimal. Mister Zang, your turn."

"Thank you, Your Honor, members of the jury," Zang's smile at the jury looked like it hurt. "We will show that the defendant was the last one to see the victim before her death. And lastly, the defendant was jealous that the madam was entitled to half of the defendant's earnings without lifting a finger."

"We have seen that almost all of the possible suspects have walking and talking alibis that clear them from the scene of the murder. First and foremost, A.J. Tully, who's ten thousand dollars went into financing Misses DuPaulette's New Year's Eve party. The money went to buying part of the French champagne and Misses DuPaulette's party gown. That investment made Mister Tully an obvious suspect. The problem was that Mister Tully was in Denver for a week before the murder. In fact, he met the defendant's lawyer on the train from Denver. I suspect the defendant's lawyer would be a good alibi."

"Next the Woodward Brothers. Fred, who did not go to the party because he is a Baptist and married. I'm not sure which took precedent, but for sure he was not at the party." District Attorney Zang grinned at his little joke. "Harry was there to make business connections, and he left after dinner, which was his main reason for going to the party." Weak smile. "I understand it was a delicious dinner."

"Then we heard from Cora Hewert who worked with the defendant at the Old Homestead House but was not particularly a friend of the accused. She said that Miss Miller was prancing around like she was too good to associate with the rest of the girls.

"Those other girls views of Miss Suellen were represented by Honey B and Cozy Rosey, not their real names. They were just professional names. They said Miss Miller thought she was someone special because she got to sleep in the madam's bed. Both said Miss Miller was generally accepted by the others working for the madam, but neither could testify about Miss Miller's background because she stayed to herself most of the time.

"Then there is Ned Boatwright, a pimp. He prefers to be called a human relations agent." Some in the audience chuckled and Zang smiled coyly. "Madam Opal DuPaulette had taken out a loan from Mister Sullivan. She paid him back each week with money from Old Homestead business income. Rather than having a woman carrying money around town and up to Money Mountain each week, DuPaulette and Sullivan arranged to have a messenger carry the money, Mister Boatwright. Later in the week DuPaulette would go to

Sullivan for his haircut and to check that Sullivan had received the full amount, and he always had. Why? Because Mister Boatwright was an honest man and had no reason to kill Misses DuPaulette.

"That leaves Bart Rosenthal, the man sitting at the defense table, who made a spectacle of himself riding two on a horse with the defendant, Miss Miller, and otherwise cavorting around the mining district at all hours of the day and night. Despite his ostentatious behavior locally, Mister Rosenthal told me in private that he is in a serious relationship with another young lady in another town and he doesn't want her dragged into this trial. Being an honest man, I have honored his request."

"The only person who does not have a good reason for not being a suspect is the defendant, Miss Suellen Miller. Miss Miller left the party early so she could poison Misses DuPaulette's sleeping powder and then faked being asleep to avoid any suspicion of why she was in the madam's room in the first place. And why did she poison the sleeping powder? For the oldest reason there is—over money. Miss Miller killed her boss because she felt she was being taken advantage of."

The rain outside had become a quiet drizzle, and all spectators seemed spellbound by Zang's scenario as if at a play, waiting for the second act.

Coyle shuffled papers as he stood. He looked at the two occupants that shared the defendant's table with him. He gave Suellen a quick but confident smile. For Rosenthal he raised one eyebrow as if to say *What are you doing?* or possibly *Why didn't you tell me that?*

Scanning the room, Coyle started in a soft, quiet voice that somehow could be heard all across the room. Addressing the jury he said, "This closing argument will not be as long as the previous summery of what you have already heard."

At the last statement Judge Avon pulled out a handkerchief and pantomimed wiping sweat off his brow. Observers appreciated that the judge was human and still had a sense of humor.

Not sure if the joke was on him or on the DA, Coyle continued.

"What has been presented as fact as to what Miss Miller was doing between the time she left the party and when Misses DuPaulette came to the bedroom, was instead what the law calls *circumstantial* evidence. Circumstance does not carry as much weight as factual evidence. For factual evidence, I refer to the coroner's report, which was submitted as evidence number one. You will see during my closing argument how this is pertinent.

"Miss Suellen Miller is bright, levelheaded, and logical. It is a fact that Miss Miller is not well educated in book learning, although she was near the head of her class when she did attend school. We have learned that her time in school was strictly limited by her father."

"No motive has been established for Miss Miller to have murdered the only person she trusted and had a close relationship with. Mr. Zang merely offers speculation, which has no weight in the law or establishing guilt. Simply put, he's guessing because he has no hard evidence.

"At most, if Miss Miller did put poison in Misses DuPaulette's sleeping powder, it was a mistake, it was because her reading ability is very limited due to little schooling. What Misses DuPaulette claimed was harmless morphine in her jeweled case was actually a more expensive drug. That was why she did not offer to share it with anyone.

"Someone laced her sleeping powder with what they thought was cocaine, which was bad enough, but the bottle said *casaethylene,* the chemical found in rat poison. Miss Miller couldn't have read *casaethylene* or have known what it is. Was Miss Miller the last person to see the madam alive? Doubtful, because she was sleeping. I submit, and the lack of evidence shows, that Miss Suellen Miller was an innocent bystander of a murder or accident and stands accused simply because she slept in the victim's bed from time to time for innocent reasons."

Out of the corner of his eye Coyle saw Suellen dab a tear with a handkerchief. Rosenthal put a hand on her shoulder to console her.

CHAPTER 30

The jury room door had hardly been shut and Judge Avon had not even taken off his robe in his office when the jury room door flew open again and a bald head over a suntanned face peered out.

"We are ready," the man said to the sheriff's deputy guarding the door. "Can we come out now?"

"No, you can't come out until you finish your duties. You have to pick a foreman and decide guilty or not guilty. If you haven't decided by suppertime you have to come back tomorrow until every one of you agrees. Understand?"

"I am the foreman, we voted, and we agree on the verdict. Can we go home now?"

"I'll go inform the judge. Stay put until I return."

Coyle was stuffing papers and trying to keep curious lookers away from the table. Most just wanted to get a good look at the now infamous defendant. Some people stopped by to wish her good luck and then moved along.

Judge Avon was shocked by the news and quickly ordered that the court reconvene. Never had a verdict in his courtroom come back within minutes.

"All the necessary parties are still in the courtroom I assume?"

"Yes, Your Honor," said the bailiff. "We've barely had time for a bathroom break."

Avon was normally stern, and stone faced. On this occasion he was clearly angry and on the edge of a temper tantrum. While everyone was getting seated, he was looking around for his gavel.

"Have you selected the foreman of the jury?"

"Yes, Your Honor, I am he . . . or him. It is I," the foreman said feeling intimidated.

"Have you reached a verdict?" the judge asked.

"We have, Your Honor."

The foreman handed the paper with the verdict to the bailiff who handed it to the judge. "Does everyone in the jury agree?" the judge asked.

"Everyone agreed even before we went to the jury room. They picked me as foreman, we read your instructions to us, and we took a vote. I even read your instructions to the couple of jurors what couldn't read so good. We understand and we agree."

Judge Avon looked skeptical. "Did all the jurors sign the verdict form?"

"Yes sir, we all signed it, including two *Xs* that I told you about." There was a slight pause. The foreman noticed Judge Avon staring at him. "Your Honor, we all agreed and signed the form, Your Honor."

"You signed the verdict before you heard the counselors' summaries and final arguments?"

"Didn't hear anything that changed anybody's mind." Slight pause. "Your Honor."

Judge Avon handed the form to the bailiff and said, "The defendant and counselor please stand."

Suellen Miller and Andrew Coyle stood. Undecided and reluctant,

Barton Rosenthal stood, too. Coyle gave him a look and then decided it wasn't worth the trouble to get Rosenthal to sit down.

The bailiff read, "The court of the City of Cripple Creek and Teller County in the State of Colorado finds the defendant, Suellen Miller, not guilty of the murder of Opal DuPaulette."

A cheer from the spectators filled the courtroom. Suellen gave Rosenthal a big hug and they walked out together getting congratulations from the crowd all the way out the door. The judge and bailiff hurried to their respective places of work. They were hoping to keep their papers in a dry place in case the roof leaked, which it did only on very rainy days or if snow was melting on the roof.

Coyle turned and to his surprise he saw Sarah weaving and pushing her way through the crowd.

"Hi, my sweet wife," Coyle said with his arms open wide.

From next to his somewhat wrinkled shirt, he heard her say, "You are the best lawyer in this town."

Coyle held Sarah at arm's length and said, "You got it wrong. I am the lawyer with the best-looking wife in this and any town."

As they walked together toward the door Sarah looked up at Coyle. "You are growing a beard. I thought you just had not shaved for a couple of days. I see how you shaped it. It is a beard."

"It will be a beard someday," Coyle smiled.

It occurred to Coyle that the reason for the beard was that Suellen liked it. She said it made him look more worldly and wise. The idea of mentioning Suellen liked the beard made Coyle choke on the words.

Thankfully, I've been married long enough to know what to say and when to not say anything.

They stood under a short awning with a small crowd trying to decide if they wanted to make a run for it. Several people left, one or two at a time. The rain showed no signs of letting up. At that instant Suellen Miller came around the corner of the building holding an umbrella.

"Oh, there you are. Hello, Misses Coyle. Mister Coyle I've been looking for you to thank you for all you have done for me." She stepped forward and Coyle froze. Suellen stuck her hand out and gave him a hearty handshake.

Coyle recovered enough to say, "Where is Mister Rosenthal? I saw you left with him."

Suellen said, "He said he ran into a cousin, but I'll bet that it's his girlfriend from Colorado Springs." Suellen winked. "Anyway, he is otherwise occupied."

Sarah said, "What a pretty, pink umbrella. Very ladylike."

Suellen nodded her thanks.

"We have visitors coming to the Old Homestead all the time and they often leave stuff behind. They've got an umbrella basket there that is plumb full. When I moved out of the house, I just grabbed an umbrella. It is pretty, isn't it?"

Sarah gave Coyle an accusing look but suddenly brightened up like she just had an inspiration. "Leona is going to be four years old on her birthday tomorrow. We are having a birthday party for her at a friend's house. And I am supposed to bake a birthday cake. Here I've got a recipe book, but I don't know what this means."

Suellen stepped onto the covered porch and handed the pink umbrella to Coyle. She took the recipe book from Sarah and found the place where Sarah did not understand.

"Take one cup of white flour and sift it into the egg and cream mixture. Sift means put in a little bit at a time. If the woman whose kitchen you are using has a flour-sifter, she can show you how to use it. Easy. If not, you can put in small amounts of flour and spread it around and mix it in before you put in a little more. When the cup of flour is all mixed into the mixture, go on to the next step. That should take care of sifting. The recipe looks like it will be good. I use butter instead of shortening."

Sarah and Coyle looked at each other. The only smile was in their eyes.

Suellen said, "If there are any questions, don't be afraid to ask."

CHAPTER 31

Katie was nearly as excited about Onie's birthday as the birthday girl herself. Katie would throw a party for her best friend's daughter.

The girls were noisily excited about the party. Sarah told them to quiet down. "You're going to wake up some of the customers at Carson's Mortuary."

"Mommy, is Mister Carson's house where they keep the dead people?"

"Just until they put them in the ground under the dirt."

"Mister Carson said we might wake them up. That would be good . . . wouldn't it?"

"He means that you are being too noisy. Would you like to help me make the frosting for your birthday cake? Can you do it quietly?"

Onie put both hands over her mouth and nodded her head.

———•◆•———

"I've invited a couple of guests," Katie said. "You can't have a party without guests."

"Good, we haven't been here long enough to have any friends

other than you and John.

"And Mable," Onie remembered to include her new best friend.

"Yes, and Mable. The guests live very close to your house that burned down," Katie said. "They have three kids, and I invited all three. "I should warn you," Katie's expression became serious, which was unusual for the happy-go-lucky child, "that the Butlers and their kids are Negroes."

Sarah laughed a not-quite-convincing laugh. "When Andrew had a case in Leadville, our landlady was Negro and we got along fine."

At that moment there was a knock at the front door. Mable ran to the door and opened it. The open door revealed three kids, and Coyle. The kids were dressed in clean and pressed clothes, but Coyle was starting to look a little rough around the edges. His days of living a bachelor's life in a hotel were starting to show.

"This is Onie, and this is her birthday." And with a grand gesture starting with the smallest, Katie introduced the three guests - "Spike, Eva, and Jerimiah. Come in, we will play some games and have some cake, and have a party. Does anyone like cake?"

"Yes, ma'am."

In the backyard, Katie took charge as the kids played a bevy of games, including a three-legged race, pin the tail on the donkey and racing through the yard in potato sacks. All laughed and were having fun.

For the three-legged race, Sarah and Eva were making good progress until Sarah fell over Mable and Onie. Sarah's full-length skirt blew up to her knees in the fall. She busily tried to straighten her skirt while her partner was still trying to run. Sarah had not shown her knees in public before.

Coyle struck up a conversation with his three-legged race partner. "How old are you Jerimiah?"

Jerimiah held up nine fingers.

"Nine? I was guessing ten or maybe eleven. You are big for your age."

"Yes, sir. My whole family is big, sir. My father got schooling so he don't have to do heavy work. He wants me to do good in school, so I don't have to do muscle work either. Use my head not my back. Work like you do, sir."

"You better find a better example to use as a sample of the kind of life you want to live." Coyle chuckled.

Jerimiah looked puzzled. "Example and sample. They do rhyme?" Before Coyle could think of a way to explain what he was trying to say, the boy jumped up.

At cake-eating time, Coyle found himself next to Jerimiah and decided to continue their conversation. "Your father is right. Most of the time, it is better to use your head instead of your muscles. But sometimes muscles are a good thing. Where does your father work?"

"Your wife makes good birthday cake, yumm. My daddy is a conductor on the Colorado Springs to Cripple Creek run."

"A conductor, Mister Butler, I talked with him in court the other day. I asked him if a friend was on the train one certain night. And he remembered my friend was on the train to Colorado Springs. It kept my friend out of trouble."

"Your wife makes good cake, Mister Coyle. I wish Onie had a birthday every day."

"Here, you can have my piece of cake. I didn't touch it. I was talking to you. Have some more cake, please."

"Thank you, sir. My daddy was a good witness, wasn't he?"

"Yes, he was." Coyle smiled. "How would you like to work with me finding evidence?"

"Yes, I would like that."

"Okay, I'll check with your father, Jerimiah." Coyle liked the boy already, but he wished he hadn't given away his cake.

Onie came around the table to talk to Sarah. "How come it is called frosting and it isn't even cold?"

Katie beat Sarah to the punch. "Frosting isn't cold like frost on the window in the winter. They ran out of names for things." Katie shook a little when she laughed. "They could have named it snow, but frosting sounds better like butter on toast and frosting on cake."

Sarah felt a little uncomfortable. It was the first time her daughter had asked a question that Sarah could not answer. *So, this is what four is going to be like* was written all over her face.

CHAPTER 32

Coyle looked over at Jerimiah Butler. He was dressed in a pressed purple and yellow striped shirt. Jerimiah was smiling and Coyle could not help smiling back at that smile.

"Has your father taken you on his train before?"

"Oh, lots of times." Jerimiah looked out the train window and then back at Coyle. "Well, a couple of times, sir. He's very busy when the train is moving, taking tickets and things. Keeping riders happy. He is on the evening run to the Springs and I ain't allowed to stay up that late. Daddy says when I talk to you, I'm supposed to tell the truth, the whole truth and nothing but the truth."

"That is the best idea when you are talking to anyone. Now that we're working together, Mister Jerimiah Butler, we will look for tracks or something that is out of place or has been moved. I'll give you a nickel. If you find something that looks like a clue, I'll give you a dime."

"Your daddy was very kind to let you come help me," said Coyle.

"Mama didn't want to let me go with you because you been shot at twice."

"How did she know that?"

"Mama is good friends with Jodeanna who cooks at the Lewis

house in Colorado Springs. Jodeanna heard from the Lewises who heard from Mister Rosenthal who knows everything about you."

"Tell your mother and father that if there is any shooting, the shooter will be shooting at me, and you will be safe. And Mister Rosenthal doesn't know everything."

"Yes, sir."

"We are not trying to catch somebody doing something wrong."

"No, sir."

"We are lookin' for evidence. Evidence is a thing that tells us what happened and if we know what happened, it will help up to find who did it."

"Yes, sir."

"The sheriff thinks I killed someone, so we should look for some evidence that proves I didn't do it. Understand?"

"No, sir."

"You will be okay. You have been hunting up here. Just look around and tell me if you see something that doesn't look right. I don't know what that might be."

"Yes, sir."

Victor was the end of the line and Coyle and Jerimiah set out to look for evidence, whatever and wherever that might be.

"Over there are the baseball stands where they held the bullfight. Did you go to the bullfight?"

Jerimiah chuckled. "No, sir, my father and mother said it was too cruel. The bull had no chance. It was the first time they agreed on something."

"I bet there were other things upon which they agreed."

Jerimiah picked up a stone and threw it. "Yeah, me and some friends played bullfight. I always had to be the bull because I am the biggest. They took turns being the matador. They had towels that

I was supposed to charge when they swung them and stood like a matador. Clyde got to go to the bullfight, so he knew how to stand. But I was smarter than a bull and sometimes I ran over them. My mother and father both said me and my friends were being silly. They agreed on that."

"Sometimes being silly is fun," Coyle said. "Grownups do it all the time."

They walked from the playground toward the train station on a path the Coyles had taken on their way back to the train to Cripple Creek.

"Here is the place where I was standing while we tried to get ready to catch the train back to Cripple." Coyle pointed at a grove with aspen and pines. "So, I want to go over to those trees and look for evidence. Anything might help. Where the shooter was standing, broken limbs on the bushes, maybe the shooter dropped something. Can you help me?"

"Yes, sir, we are looking for evidence."

They marched over thirty to forty yards to the grove and looked around. Under bushes, around some boulders, everywhere in their path. Coyle found that Jerimiah was good at looking for signs of disturbances because of his hunting days. Coyle thought he found something. It turned out to be some rabbit scat and not much of it. Jerimiah enjoyed that but didn't show it. He thought it might be a case of a grownup acting silly.

After a short distance they found a big rock lodged against a pine tree. Under one side of the rock there was a rabbit hole. They both laughed. A few minutes later Jerimiah yelled that he found something.

"Over here, I think this is evidence . . . sir."

"Another rabbit hole," Coyle teased.

Jerimiah stood over a spent rifle shell. He pointed proudly.

"You sure did find some evidence," Coyle said as he stooped down. He put the shell in an old cigar case he had brought for this very reason.

"The bullet shell will be good evidence for you?" Jerimiah was clearly proud of himself, and he smiled when Coyle handed him a dime and a compliment.

They walked a few yards farther and found a pile of horse excrement. "You don't want to put that in your pocket, do you?" Jerimiah chided.

"No, I want to put it into your pocket," said Coyle as he made a false move toward Jerimiah who froze with a big grin. They both laughed. We better get back to the train station. We have another stop to make before we go home."

CHAPTER 33

The train engineer didn't have any problem making the unscheduled stop at the Independence Mine. He would be more surprised if he didn't have to make a stop there. What did surprise him was seeing Coyle get off with a young Black boy. Thought to himself, *The boy was probably caught playing hooky or something. Oh well, let Mister Coyle worry about it.* The train pulled away on its way back to Cripple Creek.

"We will look around here for more evidence. Maybe, the same person who shot at me and missed, shot at Mister Sullivan, and didn't miss. Jerimiah was more animated now that he knew what evidence was and that he had found some.

They looked high and low around Sullivan's cabin. Coyle took the windows and Jerimiah looked for bullet shell casings and footprints in the dirt around the cabin to no avail, but the dirt was pounded down by dozens of shoes and boots.

After Coyle was satisfied that the windows were intact and it would be impossible to see a bullet hole in the logs, he tried the door. As expected, there was a notice on the door that the mine was closed until details of the mining claim could be straightened out at the Colorado mining office.

That was when Coyle heard the first shot. He ducked and looked around. He could see where the bullet hit. Nothing was disturbed. Then he saw a purple blur in the tall grass between the mine and the train track at the bottom of the hill. Another shot. The purple blur dropped out of sight.

"No, no, that's just a boy!" Coyle ran down the stairs from the front door and down the hill to the place where he had last seen the purple shirt.

"Are you okay? Where does it hurt?"

Coyle hugged the boy to his chest and looked around. Not seeing anyone he loosened his bear-hug on the intended target. Jerimiah smiled ear to ear.

"Daddy said if anyone shoots at me, to fall down and play dead."

"You sure fooled me. Let's look at that shirt." He looked at the purple and yellow striped shirt until he came to a hole in the shirt tail.

"Did you get hit?"

"No, I was hot and left the shirt tail out to cool off."

"Just tell your mother that you tore the shirt climbing a tree when you were looking for evidence." Coyle said. "Truth, the whole truth and the nothing but the truth."

Jeremiah stood with his arms folded across his chest.

Coyle smiled. "You've right. Tell your mother and father I'm sorry and I had no idea anybody was going to take a shot and especially not at you. And for telling the truth, here is another dime and I'll buy you a new shirt too."

"Okay."

"Let's walk down the train tracks to the next station at the Frisco mine. The train stops there. You can look for evidence on the way. I think the shooter went that way."

———◆———

The two followed the railroad tracks and the horse signs next to the railroad down the hill to the station where the sheriff and his deputies had captured Coyle. It was a quiet walk. Coyle was thinking and Jerimiah was looking for evidence. As they came into sight of the Frisco the hoof prints veered away from the railroad station to the high sage and grass.

Jerimiah wanted to follow the horse tracks, hoping they would lead to more evidence.

"No," Coyle said. "The shooter might be hiding somewhere along the way and take a shot at us." He paused a few minutes, then added, "We don't need any more shooting our way, do we?"

"Nope."

Coyle didn't know what happened to "no sir" and "yes sir," but he was glad they could now talk like partners.

The train whisked them back to Cripple Creek. Coyle was never as glad to get off of Money Mountain and back to the Creek. Next, he had to face Misses and Mister Butler. *That can't be any worse than having somebody shooting at their son.* Coyle thought. *A stop at the general merchandise store might make the meeting a bit more cordial.*

"Hello, Misses Butler. I brought Jerimiah home in good shape. Good as new as they say." Coyle chuckled unconvincingly.

Jerimiah joined in with, "I found some evidence, and we followed the shooter's horse hoof prints until he went off the trail. 'Cause he might have been waiting behind a tree and ambushed us. And Mister Coyle bought me a new shirt 'cause the shooter shot a hole in mine."

Misses Butler grabbed Jerimiah and hugged him. "Where did he shoot you? You got to go to the doctor." She turned her knife-like stare toward Coyle.

Coyle responded with, "And shoes, too."

Misses Butler exploded. "You think a new shirt and a pair of shoes will take the place of my son? You said nobody's going to get shot. Most of all not my boy. It would be safe."

"Mama, Mister Coyle didn't know. We didn't see anybody at the mine. I was lookin' for evidence and walked into a bushwhack. The shooter shot a hole in my shirt, see?" He held up his old shirt and put a finger through the hole.

Misses Butler answered with a torrent of nonstop tears.

Jerimiah said, "My Father is at work getting ready for the night runs of the train to the Springs, he'll understand."

"You might need to go to court to tell what you saw. Remember everything that happened today. Write it down if you need to. You are very brave." He turned to Misses Butler. "Jerimiah is a good boy and brave. I am sorry I put him in danger. Thank you."

CHAPTER 34

The date of Coyle's trial was fast approaching, and the lawyer had not tried to line up someone to testify that he couldn't have killed Winston Sullivan. Even his friends like Rosenthal, and Bart's future in-laws, the Lewis family, or Bart's business partner, A.J. Tully, gave him funny looks as they met him on the street. Suellen Miller, if that was her real name, which was doubtful, had moved out of the Palace Hotel and went back to the Old Homestead boarding house.

In the meantime, Coyle made a crude sketch of the horseshoe print that he and Jerimiah had seen in the sand and then tracked when they left Sullivan's cabin. The shooter's horse had a distinctive mark on the shoe. Coyle made a mark on the sketch where the horseshoe was nicked. His other evidentiary tidbit was the .44 caliber shell casing Jerimiah had found.

It was a fine early spring day in Cripple Creek. The mud had mostly dried. New brick buildings were replacing the wooden buildings lost in the fires. *Ahhh, the bricks and mortar*, Coyle thought. *Anyone who says bricks don't have a smell has not been to a recently rebuilt downtown.*

There were two livery stables in Cripple, and the second one Coyle visited paid off with the information he needed.

"Did Suellen Miller rent a horse Tuesday?"

"Fine looking woman. I wouldn't forget her. Or for that matter, I couldn't afford her either. I've got it right here. I keep track of when they check out and what time they bring the animal back." The stable man held up his rental ledger. "Tuesday, half a day. Actually, I gave her twenty minutes before noon for free and she brought the horse back early anyway, so it was a wash. Looked good even in those men's clothes she was wearing."

"Would you testify to those times and the date in court and under oath?"

"It is right here in the log. No need to lie."

"I'll see you in court, Mister Adams. And the young lady won't be wearing men's riding clothes."

The next stop was the sheriff's office to make sure Coyle knew what was coming.

"Howdy, Sheriff. Got your ducks in a row?"

"Good day, Mister Coyle. Do you mean do we have the witnesses lined up?" Sheriff O'Malley dipped his finger into his pouch of chewing tobacco and took a whiff. "Nasty stuff. I just keep it around because it gives me confidence to know that it is there if I need it."

"What does that have to do with getting ducks in a row?" Coyle quipped.

"The DA takes care of the row, makes sure it is straight and all. And I take care of the ducks. Some of them won't show up, but we have enough of them to show that you walked down from Sullivan's cabin, and you were the last one to see him alive. We can't convince witnesses that the system won't work if they don't follow the law."

Coyle removed a handkerchief from his pocket. He unwrapped the little bundle to expose a bullet shell. Sheriff O'Mally reached for the shell. Coyle said, "Don't touch it, Sheriff, it might have fingerprints."

"I know that," O'Malley responded. "You think I'm some kind of an idiot?"

Coyle discounted the first few answers that came to mind.

Sticking a pencil in the open end of the shell, Coyle handed over the pencil and the shell. "What caliber is it and what fired it?"

With a couple of quick sniffs and a ceremonial waving of the pencil and shell under his nose which was reminiscent of a waiter testing wine samples in a glass, the sheriff announced his verdict. "It is not a recently shot shell, but not more than two weeks old. Definitely a Winchester rifle .45 caliber. So?"

"So, we'll see what the jury will think of that in court."

Sheriff O'Mally chuckled good-naturally and said, "Just in case there is a run on jail cells this weekend, we've got a special one reserved for you."

After leaving the sheriff's office, Coyle headed back to the Palace Hotel. He got a feeling somebody was following him. He slowed and the person behind did the same. The same when he quickened his pace.

Suddenly Coyle turned around. The person behind him ran into Coyle and they both teetered, almost falling. Coyle caught his pursuer's arm to keep him from toppling.

"You're a deputy sheriff, are you not?"

"Just part time when I'm not prospecting. And sometimes when there is a special case."

Coyle thought for a minute. "You think I'm a special case?"

"Sheriff O'Mally said he has never set an accused murderer loose to run around town trying to prove he didn't do it."

Letting go his grip on the man's arm, Coyle said, "You go on back to the sheriff and tell him I wouldn't miss the trial for anything. I want to see if we can discover who did murder Mister Sullivan, and I'll prove it wasn't me."

CHAPTER 35

Court was held in what once had been a vacant warehouse. It was sprawling and sterile and selected by the county commissioners when Cripple Creek became the county seat of Teller County in 1899.

Judge George Knox was brought in from Colorado Springs to ensure a fair trial. That suited Coyle just fine; out of town sounded better to him than a local person with local ties and relationships presiding over his guilt or innocence.

R.A. Zang, the defeated assistant DA, was tapped to prosecute Coyle, presumably because he had learned many of the facts of the case against Coyle in the Miller trial. On the other hand, Coyle also suspected a desire for revenge as being part of Zang's motivation.

The defense attorney unfortunately was going to be Coyle himself. He thought he knew and understood the drawbacks of that strategy. He wouldn't have Rosenthal or Suellen Miller sitting beside him for support, either. He was convinced that Suellen's good looks had a lot to do with the not guilty verdict by the all-male jury. He thought he would need some of that magic in this trial.

The jury selection went well, even though Coyle didn't recognize any members of the pool. He asked each candidate if they were sheriff's deputies. He also asked if they served as volunteers on any posse for the sheriff, particularly the posse that brought him in from the Frisco train station. None of those Coyle selected had been on the posse that brought Coyle back to the Creek, and only two had served on a jury in the last six months.

Apparently being on a posse is a part-time job for many of the men in Cripple Creek, Coyle concluded.

Zang asked if they were married, and if they were single, were they customers of the Old Homestead. It was an odd question, but most of married men seemed relieved that the DA did not ask them the second part of the two-part question.

Coyle thought Zang's questions indicated that he was trying to keep the members of the jury on his side by sparing them any embarrassment.

———◆———

Zang made his case. Evidence leaned on the fact that Coyle had met with Sullivan and afterward walked away to the Frisco train station rather than waiting at the Independence's pull-off for loading, the normal place for passengers to board the train from the Independence Mine.

Coyle gave up his chance to explain his actions except to point out that everything the prosecution said or proffered as evidence was circumstantial and, therefore, proved nothing. He then asked the judge to dismiss the case for lack of proof.

Judge Knox acted like a kid who found something worthwhile in a box of Cracker Jacks. He finally had something to say. "Denied."

———◆———

Sarah, with Onie and her friend Mable, met Coyle at the National Hotel for dinner. It was nice to get acquainted with his family again after several days of interviewing witnesses who claimed to not know nothin' about nothin'. He was starting to believe the witness candidates.

From out of nowhere, Sarah came up with, "How come Suellen Miller had my pink umbrella that you took to work that day it rained so hard? You never did explain that to my satisfaction."

"I don't remember, but it is obvious you do."

"I bet you miss walking her to court each day," Sarah said curtly. "And sitting with you at the defense table."

"She will have her day in court," Coyle said. "But this time she will be on the other side." He looked over at Onie. "Leona, how is your chicken?"

"Daddy, how come you go to work to argue? Why don't you stay at home and argue with Mama?"

"It is my job to argue. Besides, at work, sometimes I win. And at home . . . never."

Sarah looked at her children and glared snake-eyed at her husband. "At home you win only when you tell the truth."

Dinner was silent, where the only table noise came from the girls making mountains out of their mashed potatoes. Finally, while they waited for dessert, Sarah started a conversation.

"When I lived with the Lewis family, the Lewises' cook, Jodeanna, was teaching me how to cook Southern style . . . lots of ham dishes. Of course, they raise cattle and eat a lot of beef. Jodeanna cooks many chicken dishes to keep everyone happy."

"Sounds scrumptious. Wish we had a Jodeanna," Coyle jabbed.

"Stay out of jail and maybe we will someday," Sarah jabbed. "Anyway, her fried chicken is so good, crispy on the outside, and tender on the inside. Even Mister Lewis likes Southern fried chicken. But like a man, he doesn't like vegetables. Misses Lewis has a hankering for collard greens, but they have to slow cook for two hours or more, but Jodeanna doesn't put too much time into cookin' something that only one person likes."

Walking back to his hotel at the end of the evening Coyle had to admit that he did miss knowing that Suellen was just across the hall, even though he never saw her there. That he would never share with his wife.

CHAPTER 36

The next morning at court Coyle was the first one there, which was unusual because Zang had always arrived first during the Suellen Miller trial. Zang always had all of his papers laid out in neat piles and his briefcase tucked neatly under his desk.

Spectators were soon filling the pews and all jurors, twelve plus three alternates, were present in the jury room having coffee. The court reporter was getting his space set up and ready to start taking notes and his machine was all set up and ready to go. The bailiff stood at the ready by the judge's perch. Everyone was in their place—except for the prosecutor.

"All rise," called the bailiff. "Court is now in session . . ."

Zang dashed into the courtroom and to his seat, the judge peering at him with furrowed brow. Zang looked hurried, harassed, and haggard. Trailing Zang was his assistant, Homer Anderson, a recent graduate of the University of Colorado Law School.

Coyle scooted his chair to the end of the defense table as close to the prosecution as possible and winked teasingly.

"It looked like we were going to have to get the show started without you," he jabbed.

Zang whispered, "I told the kid I would meet him at the courthouse, but all he saw was this abandoned hardware store. I've been looking all over town for him. He was heading for Money Mountain. Whose side is he on, anyway?"

Coyle chuckled, looking relaxed.

Bang! The judge's mallet announced that chat time had ended.

"Let's get this dog-and-pony show underway, gentlemen, shall we?"

The morning and the better part of the afternoon was filled with an endless string of deputies swearing that they saw defendant Coyle walking down the railroad track from the Independence Mine. All of the deputies reported they had not found a gun, even though they scoured the trail back to the Independence looking for a sign. Coyle must have ditched a weapon before he reached Frisco station, some speculated to Coyle's objection.

Coyle made each witness admit that they had not found a discarded gun. Nor had they found anything to indicate that Coyle must have been carrying a gun.

The star witness for the prosecution was Sheriff O'Mally who recounted how quickly he had arrived at the scene and assembled a posse, implying his actions led to Coyle's arrest.

"Objection. The posse did not catch the defendant, me," Coyle said tapping his chest. "I did not know what was happening. I saw the posse and walked right up to the leader and inquired about why so many people were hanging around waiting for a train."

"Secondly, Sheriff O'Mally came out of the Frisco railroad station and asked me to step inside, which I did without hesitation. There was no *catching* me. I was not on the run. In fact, I had merely walked back unescorted. The prosecution's wording tends to misinterpret the whole incident."

"Objection sustained. Strike the whole part about looking for the gun and catching the defendant. The jury will forget they heard it."

Coyle's cross examination proved productive. "Your deputies didn't find any gun hidden, discarded, or abandoned. Is that true?"

"We are still looking. We will find the gun."

"How did you know Mister Sullivan had been shot?"

"A woman called on the telephone and told me," O'Mally said with belligerence.

"Did she say he was dead, or did she say he needed medical help?"

"She didn't say any more than what I told you. 'Winston Sullivan has been shot.' So, I got together a posse of men hanging around the sheriff's office, and we came to help."

Coyle stood and pondered. "So why did you go to Frisco when Mister Sullivan lived at the Independence Mine site?"

"Yes, that's true. I rounded up the posse and we rode all the way from Victor, stopping at Frisco for a minute. The front riders spotted you coming down the railroad track whistling, *Comin' Round the Mountain*. So, we just waited for you to come to us."

"Did you remember Mister Sullivan might still be alive?"

"Course I did. I made Doc Steiner a part of the posse. He took his buggy on up to the Independence to check on Sullivan while we waited for you to walk into our hands."

"And Sullivan was dead when Dr. Steiner got there?"

"You should know he was dead." Sheriff O'Mally used a clean handkerchief to polish his glasses.

"Objection. The sheriff answered more than I asked by putting an opinion in his answer."

"Sustained. No opinions, Sheriff O'Mally. Just answer the questions."

The next witness was Dexter Butler representing his son Jerimiah, who had to go to school to keep his perfect attendance record intact. Dexter had to testify early in the afternoon because he had to go to work to get the train ready for its evening runs, one of the duties of the conductor the public seldom sees. After he was sworn in, Zang yielded to Coyle.

"Mister Butler, you testified in the Opal DuPaulette trial. Is that correct?"

"Yes, sir, I did."

"Yes, you did a good job and were very helpful. Did you discuss why your son, Jerimiah was helping me to investigate?"

"Yes, sir. He said he was looking for evidence that you might not see on the ground. He said, 'Four eyes are better than two when you are look'n for evidence.'"

"Those are his words, not yours, is that true?"

"Yes, sir. He is pretty smart."

"Smart indeed. Did he find any evidence?"

"Just that bullet shell," Butler said.

Coyle unwrapped a bullet shell from a handkerchief and put a pencil through the open end from where the bullet had exited. He held it up and then took the evidence to the judge's table.

The bailiff wrote a note and then placed the shell, pencil, and handkerchief on the note. He announced, "Exhibit A had been entered."

"No more questions, Your Honor."

"No questions for now," Zang said, "but I reserve the right to recall the witness should other information become available."

On his way past the defense table, the prosecutor leaned over and whispered to Coyle, "Misses Butler is still mad as hell for you getting Jerimiah shot at. She won't let him come near you for all the rice in China."

Coyle nodded.

"They're fine people," he said. "I can't blame her."

CHAPTER 37

The second morning, Zang and his assistant were there on time and ahead of Andrew Coyle, who strode in shortly afterward.

"Well, Coyle, you didn't take off overnight. I won that bet with the attorneys down at the office. Thank you."

Coyle didn't know if he thought that was funny or not. "Next time you bet on me, you have to split the winnings with me."

"Assuming I will win."

"If you bet on me, you'll win." Coyle, stern faced, gave no indication that he was joking.

The bailiff reported that the listed witnesses were present as were the courtroom staff. He announced Judge Knox, and they were ready to go.

———◆———

"Calling Suellen Miller."

There was a general hubbub in the audience. Women admiring Suellen's gown; men imagining what was under it. Suellen was accustomed to the attention. The same general restlessness and clammer that overcame the crowd happened every time she entered a room full of people.

After she got settled in the witness chair and arranged her ankle-length skirts, the examination began.

"Good morning, Miss Miller," Coyle started. "We worked together in the Opal DuPaulette trial. I trust you were satisfied with the results of that trial?"

"Yes, sir, I was happy."

"You will be as happy with this trial as long as you tell the whole truth and nothing but the truth. When was the last time you saw Mister Sullivan alive?"

"Saturday."

"For what purpose?"

"I offered to take over the management of the Old Homestead Boarding house." Several chuckles from the audience. "And I would pay the rest of the loan Misses DuPaulette had outstanding."

"Did he agree to your proposal?"

"He would think about it. He asked what collateral I had."

"What collateral did you say you could offer?"

Suellen smiled and adjusted her seat. "Then he said the strangest thing."

"Strangest thing?"

Suellen didn't respond.

Coyle rubbed his beard. "Please tell us exactly what Mister Sullivan said so that the jury can decide whether it was *strange*."

"Objection, there was a question but no answer," Zang said. "He is leading the witness. He asked and she didn't respond."

"Sustained, remove that question from the record," Judge Knox said. "But I would like to hear what Mister Sullivan said. Attorneys, approach the bench." Judge Knox leaned over from his desk and whispered to Suellen, "What did he say?"

Suellen whispered back, "He asked if I knew how to cut hair. I told him I used to cut my brothers' hair until they got too big to get the bowl on their heads."

Knox snickered. "The question and answer are still sustained and should be removed from the record."

"Did you rent a horse from Hoss Adams Livery two weeks ago on Saturday?" Coyle resumed.

"I don't remember." Suellen looked Coyle in the eye without any expression.

"Mister Adams keeps a record of such things. He has agreed to testify if we have any questions. He has a log of rental and names he can bring. He would be glad to come in to testify."

"I have my own log and I can check. I need to keep records for my business. But I'll take his word for it. He is a nice man. If he says Saturday, it was Saturday." Suellen raised her gloved hand slightly and gave Adams in the front row a friendly wave and a warm smile.

"Did you see my young partner, Jerimiah Butler, and I check around for evidence at Mister Sullivan's cabin on the day I named?"

"Yes, I did see two people nosing around. I was downhill from the Independence and Mister Sullivan's cabin."

"So, you were there?"

"Yes, I just said I was."

"Okay then, Miss Miller. Did you shoot at Jerimiah Butler when he was running through the tall weeds?"

"I didn't want to call attention to myself. I didn't want anyone to know about my visit to see Sullivan." Suellen's eyes narrowed and she blushed.

"So, did you shoot at him or not?'

"I didn't shoot to hurt him. I just wanted to scare him. I figured if I scared him, you would be distracted, and I could get away."

Coyle studied Suellen Miller's face without expression. "By the way, Miss Miller, what was your occupation before you came to Cripple Creek?"

"I was a sharpshooter in Buffalo Bill Cody's Wild West Show. Then Annie Oakley came along and drank whiskey with Mister Cody and Buffalo Bill didn't need me around anymore."

Coyle went to the evidence table and retrieved the shell casing and held it with a pencil through the open end. He held it up for Suellen to see, making sure the jury and audience also saw it.

"Miss Miller, can you identify the shell case as one of yours?"

"That is a .45 caliber Winchester. Mister Cody thought those guns are too heavy for women like me and Annie Oakley. Mister Cody had us using a .44 caliber 'Improved Henry.' I've still got mine."

"Did you take your 'Improved Henry' with you when you went to see Mister Sullivan?"

"A girl has to have some protection."

Coyle turned and said, "No more questions, Your Honor," as he approached his place at the defense table.

Zang jumped out of his seat, almost colliding with Coyle who was returning to his seat. "You are still under oath, Miss Miller. Why were you hanging around the Independence Mine and Mister Sullivan's cabin when you knew the mine was shut down because the owner was dead?"

"I didn't know that Mister Sullivan was dead."

"When did you know he was dead?"

"When I read the note tacked on the door, like everyone else did."

"When you left your horse and walked up to the door, you didn't know Sullivan was dead until you got close enough to read the notice on the door. Is that correct?"

"Some of the words. But I read enough to know he was dead. Yes, that is true."

Coyle had to chuckle at Zang's efforts. Suellen didn't miss a trick.

"No further questions, Your Honor," Zang said as he retreated.

The bailiff announced, "The next witness is in fact two witnesses. One can't speak loud enough to be heard in court. They both witnessed the incident in question together and the testimony of one will count as coming from both. With Your Honor's permission,"

"Unusual, but granted. Anything to get out of here quicker,"

Judge Knox said. "Bring another chair for the other witness."

The side door to an adjoining witness room opened and coming through was Marvin Goodson and, in a wheelchair, Leon Redd.

A loud gasp filled the courtroom.

"Thank you, gentlemen, for showing up. We know it was not easy for you to be here."

Redd and Goodson nodded in recognition of Coyle's greeting.

"Mister Leon Redd, was the manager of the Independence Mine and Mister Marvin Goodson was the day shift foreman of the same mine."

There was quiet applause, but Coyle spoke again before Judge Knox used his mallet for quiet. "As I remember, Mister Redd, you were talking with me in front of the office shack of the mine when we came under attack. Is that true?"

Goodson answered for Redd, "Yes."

"You were hit by a rifle bullet, correct?"

Again, Goodson answered for Redd, "He said yes." After a brief pause Goodson added, "Mister Redd said he thinks it was meant for you, but he stepped in front of you."

Coyle added, "And you and I put him on the train to the Springs, for medical care. I thank you both for the courage you showed that day." Coyle paused to applaud before carrying on. "I'm glad you made it, and Redd, I hope you recover fully."

Nods from both witnesses.

"Now we are talking about another day and another case. Do you understand?"

Nods from both witnesses.

"You were at the Independence on the day Mister Sullivan was shot?"

Redd and Goodson nodded that was correct.

"You were also aware the mine was not operating. Can you explain to me why you were there? You had no business at the mine, did you?"

There was another quick conference between Goodson and Redd. "Mister Redd wanted to recover some maps of the mine that he had made." Goodson looked at Redd for approval. Redd nodded an affirmative. Goodson continued, "Sullivan made the strike and earned the profits, but Redd followed the vein and mapped where the mine made turns and changed depth and so on. Mister Redd figured he deserved to get a couple of his maps from the manager's shack."

"Go on. What happened?"

There was another conference. "You showed up and—" pause and heavy breathing.

"Please, if the person who showed up is in the courtroom point to him or her."

Redd pointed at Coyle.

Goodson continued. "We saw you go in the cabin, Mister Coyle. You stayed there for a long time. Redd and I were afraid you would see us in the manager's shack, so we got in the elevator and lowered it enough so we could see the door of the cabin. We could almost see the door, and if you came out of the cabin, we would lower the elevator bucket and you would never see us."

"So, I did come out of the door. Tell us what happened next."

"Then you walked down the hill to the railroad track and walked away along the track toward Cripple Creek." Goodson paused and communicated with Redd.

"Mister Goodson and Mister Redd, you caught the first train out of there and went home. Am I correct?"

"No," Redd said, wheezing. He whispered the rest of his answer to Goodson, who continued.

"A man and a woman come up in a buggy and went into the cabin. That is when we skedaddled."

"Did you see the man and woman come out of the cabin?" Coyle asked.

"No, we didn't want to hang around. He was busy with his visitors. You might have noticed Redd doesn't move very fast. He was even slower then. So, we wanted to get out of there while we could."

"So, there was someone who saw Mister Sullivan alive after I left the cabin? No more questions, Your Honor."

Anderson, the assistant attorney, jumped up, "The prosecution has a question. How long did Mister Redd and Mister Goodson spend looking for the maps?"

"Nine or ten minutes." Goodson looked at Redd who gave an affirmative nod. "It didn't take long to find the maps. We were glad we missed Mister Coyle because we didn't know he was in there when we arrived."

The cross examination yielded little more information.

CHAPTER 38

"The defense recalls the witness, Cora Hewert," Coyle started. "Miss Hewert, are you comfortable?"

"Yes."

"And you took the oath to tell the truth, the whole truth, and nothing but the truth." Cora nodded, moving her lips along with the oath that she had likely recited several times in the past.

"You are the manager of the boarding house named the Old Homestead. Am I correct, Miss Hewert?"

"Yes, you might say that."

"To be clear. You are the manager, but not the owner. Can I say that?"

"The ownership is still being litigated since Opal DuPaulette has passed." Hewert straightened the new fur collar of her jacket. It was a cool day, but not that cool.

Coyle paused for a second at the word "litigated" but then continued. "And you make payments for the loan Misses DuPaulette borrowed from Mister Sullivan."

"Yes, but that is a private matter and no concern of yours," she snapped. "How did you know that?"

"Just answer the questions asked, Miss Hewert," the judge admonished.

Coyle took a wild stab at the truth.

"You and Mister Boatwright arrived in a carriage at Winston Sullivan's cabin. Isn't that true, Misses Cora Boatwright?"

"We wanted to pay him the money I owed him from the week's income."

"Was Mister Sullivan alive when you arrived?" Coyle pressed quickly to keep the witness off balance.

"Yes . . . well . . . "

"You were seen arriving by Mister Redd and Mister Goodson. You were the woman who called Sheriff O'Mally that day, were you not?"

Boatwright jumped to his feet and blurted, "You silly cow. I told you not to make that phone call!"

"I'm sorry, Ned, I wasn't sure you killed him. He could have been still alive and needed our help."

Boatwright turned to his right looking to escape. Several spectators stood to clear a path. Others were knocked out of the way. The assistant DA rushed to bring Boatwright down but tripped over a spectator.

"Take that man into custody," the judge shouted. Boatwright knocked aside a sheriff's deputy standing guard in court bullying his way toward the courtroom exit like a fullback. Sitting there just a few feet from the exit was Sarah Coyle, who during the commotion opened her handbag and grabbed the pistol loaned to her by her friend Katie.

She said sternly, "Don't move. From this distance I can't miss." The click of the revolver's hammer echoed through the courtroom as Sarah cocked the weapon.

Boatwright smiled and lurched toward her. Sarah squeezed the trigger, and the bullet went into the floor between Boatwright's two feet, causing him to jump half a hop back.

Sarah cocked the pistol again. Andrew Coyle rushed to his wife, jumping on Boatwright's back and grabbed Boatwright's striped tie. The assistant DA tackled Boatwright at the knees and pinned him to the floor while Coyle used the necktie to bind the man's ankles. A sheriff's deputy joined in the frolic and handcuffed Boatwright.

"Lock him up," the judge demanded. "And her, too," pointing to Cora Boatwright.

Sarah was sobbing. Coyle smothered his wife with kisses and carefully uncocked the revolver and dropped it into her handbag.

Judge Knox pounded with his gavel and adjourned the proceedings, retreating to his chambers.

While holding Sarah with an arm around her waist, Coyle called out, "Good work, Mister Anderson, you didn't learn to tackle like that in law school." Coyle was all grins as he used his other arm to slap Anderson on the back.

"Actually, it was taught at Yale football practice." Anderson said.

"A Yalie." Coyle slapped Anderson on the back again. "No wonder Harvard couldn't win any football games against Yale," Coyle quipped while still holding his wife.

Anderson was smiling from ear to ear. "Harvard won their share of the games, Mr. Coyle. And, well done, sir. Looks like you're a free man."

Ned Boatwright could still be heard making a ruckus while being escorted away as could his wife who was screaming, "I didn't shoot Sullivan. Boats did."

Coyle smiled at Anderson and waved back.

Outside, the crowd was dispersing in all directions. Coyle temporarily lost Sarah in the crowd. She was surrounded by strangers congratulating her for her bravery. The real jaw-dropper was that Sarah and Suellen were having a friendly conversation.

"Hi there, Mister Lawman," Sarah jumped up to get her arms around Coyle's neck. She gave him a kiss that no wife should display in public.

Katie had been hanging around outside near the courthouse with her daughter and Onie at Sarah's request.

"Daddy, you didn't have to go to jail. I'm glad this much." Onie spread her arms out wide apart.

Coyle gave Onie a big but bewildered hug.

Sarah explained, "I told Onie that you were going to have an argument at work and if you didn't win you would not come home for a long time."

Suellen joined in, "You took a big chance, you know. You have a wife and daughter counting on how well you can argue."

Sarah gestured at Suellen standing aside. "And if you didn't shoot Mister Sullivan, you would find a way to prove it in court. Suellen stood with me every day outside of the courthouse. I didn't know if you were going to come home or not. Suellen gave me hope."

"Congratulations, Mister Coyle. I knew you would win." Suellen took a quick look out of the corner of her eye and gave Coyle a quick peck on the cheek. "Sorry about the boot heel you lost at Victor baseball field. I was aiming for the dirt in front of you to kick up some dust to give you a bit of a scare. I knew you were thinking it was me that shot Sullivan. But it wasn't. I didn't want any competition when I tried to take over management of the Old Homestead. I wanted to scare you off the case. Sorry about the boot. Guess I don't shoot as good as I did with Cody's Wild West Show."

With that Suellen gave Sarah a little hug and whispered, "You better keep him. He is one of the good ones." She left and headed in the direction of the Old Homestead.

Coyle turned to Sarah and said, "She is lying. If she shot the heel off my boot, she was aiming at the heel of my boot. She doesn't miss."

Sarah said, "But she is a nice person."

Onie felt she had been out of the conversation too long, and she had something to say. "Daddy, you said you would take me to see the red lights. Miss Suellen said she knows where there are lots of red lights. Will you take us to see the red lights?"

Coyle answered in his standard non-answer answer, "We'll see."

FACTS AND RESEARCH

In my research for *Murder on Money Mountain,* I found many items that I thought would be of interest to readers, yet I did not want to write a nonfiction account. Here are a few examples of actual events that have crept into this fictional novel.

Pearl de Vera, the madame of Cripple Creek's most famous, luxurious, and expensive brothel gave a party of parties. I changed it to New Year's Eve to make it less offensive to readers. Her death has been one of the mysterious murders in Cripple Creek history.

There has been one bullfight in the US and that was in Victor, Colorado. The promoter who put on the bullfight slipped out of town afterward, leaving many unpaid bills behind.

In one week, there were two different fires that burned half the town. Led by Spencer Penrose, a committee of millionaires bought and brought in tents and food supplies to help the population live through the destruction.

Knowing a few of the facts, a reader can see that the author of *Murder on Money Mountain* has not exaggerated in describing the wild and wicked days of Colorado's last and greatest gold rush.

To learn more, see:

Money Mountain: The Story of Cripple Creek Gold
by Marshall Sprague

Cripple Creek Days
by Mabel Barbee

ABOUT THE AUTHOR

"My grandmother was the first girl born in Longmont," G. Eldon Smith bragged. By the time G. Eldon came along the population of his hometown, Longmont, Colorado, had grown to 12,000. It now stands at over 100,000 at the 2000 census.

"I prefer to write about a simpler time. A time when good was good and bad was bad."

Smith served in the Navy for five years as a photographer. He graduated from the University of Colorado at Denver with degrees in education and public administration.

He did research about test scores and job performance for the US Department of Labor and wrote test questions for the Colorado Department of Personnel for hiring and promotions. All this time his real interest was Colorado history and stories.

Smith is married. He and his wife have two dogs and live in Centennial, Colorado.

ACKNOWLEDGMENTS

Thank you, Diane Smith and Hank Tobo who were first readers and made helpful suggestions about the text. Also, I thank John Koehler and his staff at Koehler Books.

www.ingramcontent.com/pod-product-compliance
Lightning Source LLC
LaVergne TN
LVHW041942070526
838199LV00051BA/2877